A LONG TRIP TO TEATIME

When Edgar came up to it, he found the drink-seller himself laid out at length on the counter of his stall, snoring away. He was, Edgar saw with interest, a large spotted dog with trousers of hideous cut, whose long snout twitched irritably in his sleep. PAGE 42

ANTHONY BURGESS

A
LONG TRIP TO TEATIME

with twenty-one line drawings by
FULVIO TESTA

Stonehill Publishing Co.
NEW YORK

CONTENTS

CHAPTER I

Straight Through a Hole in the Desk

EDGAR WAS heartily sick of the droning voice of Mr Anselm Eadmer, who was going on, through the gorgeous spring afternoon, about Edmund Ironside and Edward the Confessor and Edward the Elder and Edward the Martyr, and the rest of the boring kings of Anglo-Saxon England. Edgar's desk was pocked with tiny holes made by doodling compass or dividers, and he thought what a capital thing it would be if he could become small enough to creep into one of those holes and vanish – his real diminished self, that was – until the lesson ended, while this big bored self became a wide-eyed responsive machine, taking it all in about Anglo-Saxon royalty. Imagine his surprise, then, to find himself suddenly on a ship being steered carefully through one of those holes – the one nearest the D of his own carved and inked-in first name – and to hear voices calling in a language he did not understand. He was standing on deck, well-wrapped against a piercing wind that cried in from the other end of the hole, and an old man was standing next to him, all white beard and oilskins, with a red-coaled pipe held firm in smiling jaws. The old man said:

'You, boy – are you on the crew-list? What's your name?

9

Solomon Eagle? John Earle? Hareton Earnscliff? Atalanta, Perseus, Cupid, Psyche, Alcestis, Pygmalion, Bellerophon? Ah, that was a great ship, the Bully Ruffian we used to call her. Speak, boy, and answer.' But he did not seem really interested, and Edgar did not wonder, for the ship had at last come through the hole, or rocky tunnel as it really was, and into a wide sea where the gulls were crying 'Repent! Repent! The end of the world is coming!'

'Eagles they should be by rights,' the old man said, still smiling. And then, suddenly frowning, he called: '*Laxdaela!*' or something like it to a couple of members of the crew, who replied with sounds like *isk* and *bosk* and *etheldeth*. 'We put you ashore,' said the old man to Edgar, 'on Easter Island. There it is, on the port bow.'

Edgar had too many questions to ask. He asked one only. 'What language are they speaking, sir?' he asked.

'There it is,' said the old man, 'coming up now. Listen to the Easter bells.' And the sea air had suddenly become alive with a sweet loud jangling. 'But don't,' he said, 'expect the place to be full of eggs and hot cross buns, because it won't. The people there have very long ears, right down to their shoulders, and their gods are the same. Look, you can see some of those stone idols, all along the shore. To keep out intruders, that was the idea. But it won't keep you out, oh dear me, no.'

'Why do I have to be put ashore?' asked Edgar. 'Why can't I stay on the ship and go wherever you are going?'

'Eastward ho,' said the old man, who, it dawned on Edgar, must be the captain. 'That's where we're going. To see Sir Petronel Flash. Also Moses and the Devil and the great Orc. No place for you, boy. Ah, the boat's being lowered.'

So it was. They were still some way from the shore, all along which stone effigies stood, and Edgar did not really enjoy

He was standing on deck, well-wrapped against a piercing wind that cried in from the other end of the hole, and an old man was standing next to him, all white beard and oilskins, with a red-coaled pipe held firm in smiling jaws.

climbing down the nets to the two rowers who awaited him, men who had stripped off their oilskins for the sudden heat and were now half-naked, though, in a sense very fully clothed in tattooings. On the chest of one of them was the blued-in face of a rather pretty girl, her presumed name Rhoda Fleming etched in beneath. 'Hallo there,' said the face, to Edgar's mixed fear and amusement. 'Vanity of vanities, all is vanity.'

'Don't you listen to her,' said the other man, whose chest and stomach were covered with a very fine map of Hindustan, all twinkling lights and bullock-carts moving along the roads. 'It's for me she's saying that, not you. What you might call a long-standing feud, my name being Bob Eccles. So, then – off we go.' And they both plied lustily with their oars. The man who had not yet spoken now spoke, though jerkily and rather breathlessly with the effort of rowing:

'You watch out, son, for the mother of the Blatant Beast. If you see a lady there that's like a big snake from the waist down, then you know it's her.'

'No, no,' cried Edgar with sudden panic. 'Take me back. Take me back to school and Mr Eadmer and the kings of Anglo-Saxon England.'

The two men laughed, and Rhoda Fleming laughed too, all blue teeth.

'Why,' said Bob Eccles, 'bless your heart, son, she's nought to be afeared on. Worn out she is now, having been mother to no end of monsters – Chimera and Orthrus and the Sphinx of Egypt itself. Also Cerebo and the Hydrant.'

'Haven't got them two last ones quite right,' said the other man. 'But never mind. Sing us a song, young un, to keep us in trim for the rowing.' So Edgar sang a song he knew, when he started, he did not know, but knew that he would know when he started. It went like this:

But by now the two little blue-clad men were jumping up and down on the very edge of the pier and crying: 'The pancakes are burnt and it's all your fault.'

> *'A forrard leak on the garboard strake*
> *And the harbour bar o'erflowing,*
> *For there's many a man must whistle and ache*
> *And stretch and stitch till his callions break,*
> *And hark to the cock for the morning's sake*
> *And his cree cray crack craw crowing.'*

To, but perhaps not really, his surprise, the two toiling mariners joined in with a shanty burden:

> *'With a hey and a ho and the bo'sun's dead*
> *And his bed unmade in the morning.'*

Edgar found himself, without effort, trolling a second verse:

> *'The trisail's brayed on the mizzen trees,*
> *And sop up rum by the bottle,*
> *And the galley's alive with the reek of cheese,*
> *And the noontide lobscowse fails to please,*
> *And the cargo's eaten alive by fleas,*
> *And the donkey goes half-throttle.'*

The two rowers growled their refrain:

> *'With a hoo and a hee and the first mate's oiled*
> *And he's boiled with eggs in the morning.'*

To his, but he was no longer really capable of it, surprise, Edgar found that he was being rowed towards a nice clean wooden pier, and two little men in blue uniforms were dancing up and down on it, as if with rage at the approach of the boat.

'What's that they're shouting?' Edgar asked.

Both rowers made faces, as if to say: it's always like this. The one who was not Bob Eccles said: 'It's their dinner-hour, you see, and they don't like to be disturbed at it.'

'*In it,*' the other said, 'or perhaps *during it* might be more of an ecclesiastical polity.'

'No, more of an ecclesiastical sonnet, I'd say,' said the other, and the tattooed face of Rhoda Fleming began to recite

14

I wandered lonely as a cloud. 'Not having that I'm not,' said her owner sadly, looking down and giving himself three extra chins. 'It's the mention of Wordsworth that does it,' he explained to Edgar. 'She met him once, you see when I was having a bath in Lake Windermere, if you know where that is. Silly old man, I thought, with his top hat on.'

'Look,' Edgar said, as the boat began to touch the steps of the pier, 'why don't they get on with having their dinner instead of jumping up and down like that in a rage?'

The other two shook their heads. 'See now,' said the one who was not Bob Eccles, 'why don't I give my name so as you'll know it? It happens to be Boniface, if you're at all by way of being the least mite interested. Some say as it's really Bonny Face and others as it's really Bony Face, but there's not one bone in my etchy omo as you can see, save for the sniffer perhaps, so I plump for the other meaning.'

'Your what?' asked Edgar.

'His sniffer,' answered Bob Eccles. 'Or his honk or hooter or else his maundy thursday.'

'No, no, the other one.'

But by now the two little blue-clad men were jumping up and down on the very edge of the pier and crying: 'The pancakes are burnt and it's all your fault,' whereupon Boniface yelled:

'I don't believe you're having pancakes, today being Wednesday.' Surprisingly, or not so, this quietened them down a good deal, so that one of them said to Edgar:

'All right, let's be having you up then.' And they quite kindly helped Edgar as he came to the top of the pier-steps, one of them saying: 'You can come a nasty crack there when it's all slimy with the sea-slime and the outcroppings of the topmore gudgeons.' Boniface called up:

'Don't forget to tell them now where you want to go.'

'But I want to go where I've come from,' cried Edgar in some distress 'I want to be in school for the end of the lesson and then be ready to go home to tea.'

'Tea,' and one of the blue-clad men shook his head, saying: 'You'll have to go a good way inland to see about tea. Where the Exhibition is if the truth is to be told, and a good fair crack to the feet it is to get there. But let's be having you in the office.' And Edgar noticed that there was a little hut a hundred yards or so along the pier, from which loud screams were coming. The two sailors started to pull back towards the ship, which seemed to have travelled on a good number of sea-miles without waiting for them, singing:

'With a hoy and a haw and the skipper's fried
And he's tied with springs in the morning.'

'Now,' said one of the blue-clad men, 'let's have a look at you.' Edgar had a look at *them*. Their hair was very fine and very wild in the sea wind and their noses very red. They seemed, each of them, to be no more than about three feet in height, but they were so paunchy that their blue jackets were made to fit with a loop of string between button and buttonhole. 'Well, now,' said the one who was speaking, 'you seem to be a fair upstanding specimen of a recantation, and I'll thank you to know that I'm Mr Eckhart and this one is called Mr Eckermann.'

'You're Germans?' Edgar asked politely.

'No,' thundered back Mr Eckhart, 'we're brothers.'

'But I don't understand that,' said Edgar. 'I mean, you have different names. If you were brothers, you'd have the same name.'

They both roared with laughter. 'Ah,' cried Mr Eckermann, 'little you know of the great world, and that's a fact. Brothers have to have different names, otherwise you couldn't tell them apart. Suppose Cain and Abel had had the same name,

'Well, as for money, the time's arrived. Come on, don't waste it.
To the office.' And they hurried off, Edgar following, the seagull
now on Mr Eckermann's head and calling 'Liddell and Scott,
Liddell and Scott.' But when they came to the little hut it flew off,
craaaarking, into the sea wind.

eh? That would have made a pretty mess for everybody.' And they both chuckled. Mr Eckhart at last said:

'Not that this is the job our father would have chosen for either of us. I did a great thing once upon a time. I used to go around warning people about monsters, but they'd never listen.'

'Ah,' Edgar said, 'like the Blatant Beast and its mother?'

'Well, sometimes,' Mr Eckhart said doubtfully. 'But it was more what they call Venus, she being what was known as the goddess of love, whatever that is or was.'

'A lot of nonsense,' Mr Eckermann said. 'Me, I was a great one for the conversations, but that's all over now, aye aye, all over.' They both looked so sad, even though a seagull had landed on the head of Mr Eckhart and was crying 'Eclectic electric eccentric', that Edgar thought he had better remind them that there was work to be done in what they called the office, from which the screaming still came. He said:

'The trouble is I have no money.'

'Money money money,' Mr Eckhart grumbled. 'That's all anybody thinks about.' He looked at his wristwatch, from which a very subdued kind of singing seemed to be coming, and said: 'Well, as for money, the time's arrived. Come on, don't waste it. To the office.' And they hurried off, Edgar following, the seagull now on Mr Eckermann's head and calling 'Liddell and Scott, Liddell and Scott.' But when they came to the little hut it flew off, craaaarking, into the sea wind.

The hut was very small and very untidy. The screaming, Edgar now saw, was not coming from anybody being hurt but from a parrot with a little silver ring about its left leg, attached to a thin chain that was attached to a tall hatstand. The hat-stand was crammed with every possible kind of headgear, from concertina-folding opera-hat to Sherlock Holmes deerstalker, and all were quite clearly too big for either Mr Eckhart or Mr

Eckermann, and far far far too big for the little man who sat behind a desk in great gloom, eating some very sticky-looking and rubbery candy from a paper bag. He had a long nose like an empty ice-cream cone with a pencil attached to its apex, and this was all covered with candy, so that he had to keep wiping it with a very grubby handkerchief. 'It's a terrible burden to be sure,' he said, 'eating of this.' The parrot screamed very loudly from the crown of a bowler hat, but nobody took any notice. Mr Eckermann, or it might have been Mr Eckhart, said petulantly:

'Why didn't you make cocoa, as you were asked and as is your duty?'

'It's no good making cocoa, nor drinking it neither,' said the little man, 'since the spoon keeps getting into your eye.' And then he became very official, looking sternly at Edgar, putting the bag of candy into a desk drawer. Out of the drawer something invisible seemed to fly out for Edgar heard a tiny voice call:

'Aye aye. I. Eye.'

'Passport,' said the little man, 'and quick about it.'

'Titititit,' went the little voice. It was now near the parrot, and the parrot looked at it, its head on one side.

'You've let the echo out,' said Mr Eckermann or Mr Eckhart sternly. 'You've been warned about that often enough.'

'Nuff nuff nuff.'

'It does nobody any good, having it,' went the little man gloomily. He wore, under his blue jacket, a rainbow-striped jersey that Edgar rather liked the look of, though it would be much too small for himself to wear.

'The time's coming up for the race,' Mr Eckhart or Mr Eckermann said.

'Ace ace ace.'

'Now you have to place your bet,' Mr Eck said (it was easier this way, decided Edgar). 'Put your money in that letter-box there,' and he gestured with his nose towards a beautifully polished brass letter-box mouth in the wall.

'But I have no money,' Edgar said, 'as I told you.'

'I'll lend him a couple of hamadans,' said the other Mr Eck, taking some bright small coins from his jacket pocket. 'After all, it's what they call, or used to call in the days of my youth, a foregone conclusion.'

'Usion usion.'

So the money was put into the letter-box, and the other Mr Eck said to the parrot: 'Eclipse first and the rest nowhere.'

The parrot listened very carefully and, it seemed to Edgar, seriously to that, its head on one side, and it crooned to itself.

'What is this?' asked Edgar. 'Eclipse, I mean.'

The little man spoke. 'The most famous race-horse in the world it is, and running today in the Queen's Plate at Winchester. Born during an eclipse it was, and so hence, notwithstanding, and not to put too fine a point on it, its name.'

'Ame ame ame.'

'Quiet now,' said one of the Mr Ecks. 'Shut that echo up.'

'Up up up.'

Everybody was now quiet, and the Mr Ecks looked at each other in triumph, since the echo had, indeed, shut up. The parrot seemed to be listening to something intently. After about a minute it began to flap its wings and dance up and down. The little men, all three of them, looked gravely at each other.

'Won,' said one of the Mr Ecks. Echo agreed, three times.

'How do you know?' Edgar asked.

'It always wins,' said the little man. 'Never lost yet. Ah, here comes the money.' And out of the letter-box came the two coins, followed by the smallest coin that Edgar had ever seen. All three tinkled onto the floor.

'Can't win much, you see, it stands to reason,' said Mr

Eck. 'It always comes in first, always has done, always will. Anyway, those two hamadans go back to us, and you can keep the vathek, not worth much but better than nothing.'

'Thing thing thing.'

'Thank you,' Edgar said, pocketing the tiny coin they called a vathek. The little man at the desk said:

'Anything to declare?'

'What do you mean?' asked Edgar.

'You answer the question. You're bringing things into the country, and you have to say what they are. And some things you have to pay money on.'

'But you can see,' Edgar said, 'I have nothing.' And he held out his hands as if to show that there was nothing hidden in them.

'You're a bit of a liar,' said one of the Mr Ecks. 'You have that vathek in your pocket.'

'All right, then. I declare that.'

'Not enough,' said the other Mr Eck. He went over to a corner of the room, brushing the echo out of the way irritably as he did so. There was a load of old rubbish in the corner – bucolics and eclogues and barclays and sylviuses and economics and bagehots and darwins and ector and kays and seneschals, all very dusty. He came out with a big dusty carpet-bag and began stuffing it with hats from the rack. The parrot danced and squawked, and echo squawked too, so that the parrot put his head on one side to listen, but by this time there was nothing to hear. Mr Eck gave the stuffed bag to Edgar and said: 'Now.'

'Ow ow ow.'

'Anything to declare?' asked the little man at the desk.

'Just this,' Edgar said.

'Confiscated. How dare you try to bring all those hats into the country.' And he began to throw the hats back on to the rack, missing several times to the great glee of the parrot. Very grimly, he said: 'I suppose you've no passport, either.' He began to rummage crossly in the drawer that the echo had flown out of. 'No good, no good,' he kept saying. 'There's nothing here that suits. This passport's for a young girl from the depths of Manchester, by the name of Edda de Maris, and this one's for an old man by the malory of Snorri Sturlason, from Trinitaria he is, so neither will do.'

'Do do do.' The echo was now right on top of the desk. The little man shot out his hand, closed it, and cried:

'Got it. In there with you, my lady.' And he put an invisibility into the drawer, then closed the drawer. 'So,' he said gloomily again. 'It looks as if we'll have to let you in without a passport.'

'Thank you,' Edgar said. 'And how do I get home in time for tea?'

Messrs Eckermann and Eckhart said together: 'We know nothing of tea here. It's cocoa we drink.' The parrot screamed and screamed at Edgar. 'Who are you waiting for, boy?' said the little man behind the desk. 'We've done our duty by you as none can deny, so on your way to wherever you're going.'

'Sing him your song to cheer him on his way,' said one of the Mr Ecks.

'Oh, all right then,' grumbled the little man, and he sang grumpily while the parrot screamed an accompaniment:

'Sir Arthur Stanley Eddington
(1882 to 1944)
was educated at Owens College, Manchester,
And Trinity College, Cambridge,
And was professor of astronomy at Cambridge
And was a distinguished astronomer,
Noted for his researches into the
Stellar system and the internal

They were mostly quite small, and one little man had two dogs which were much bigger than himself. He kept hitting one of them with a feeble little hand, crying 'Naughty naughty', but the great beast, it was clear, did not even feel the blow.

Constitution of stars,
Also for his contributions
To the theory of relativity
And the popularization of
Modern physical theory.'

As that seemed to be the end of the song, Edward said:
'Thank you very much. That was delightful.'

'Delightful?' said Mr Eck. *'Delightful?* Stella Cistern was
one of the most beautiful girls in the world.' They all now turned
their backs on Edgar, including the parrot, so he left the office and
went out into the sea wind. 'Constitution of Staaaaaars,' cried the
gulls.

CHAPTER II

Eden

EDGAR WALKED towards the land. The pier led to a long street which stretched left and right as far as the eye could see, and it was full of pleasant-looking houses painted very richly – red and orange and yellow and even purple – and people were seated outside their front doors in little gardens, sunning themselves. They waved quite amicably to Edgar as he stood, his back to the sea, wondering which way to go. They were mostly quite small, and one little man had two dogs which were much bigger than himself. He kept hitting one of them with a feeble little hand, crying 'Naughty naughty', but the great beast, it was clear, did not even feel the blow. Looking up, Edgar saw a signpost which said: TO EDEN. There was no signpost giving other instructions, so it was to Eden he decided to go. As he started off, turning right to do so, a little old woman, fanning herself with a newspaper on a chair in her garden, called:

'Going to Eden, is that it, young man?'

'How far is it?' asked Edgar.

'It gets further every day,' she said. 'It's a question of the Expanding Universe, you know. But you should be there by nightfall if you don't dawdle.'

Edgar thanked her and began to walk. As the view of the sea on his right was rather monotonous, he crossed over, coming, as he walked on, to a number of little shops which sold canned gavestons, toy woolly lambs, strawberry isabellas, and other interesting objects. And then he came to a baker's shop where a fat old woman was crying with pain because, as she told the whole world (though the whole world was not there to hear her, only a very thin man with a goatee, chewing and chewing) she had burned her hand in putting some loaves into the oven. The man said to her:

'It's not possible, right? There's no such thing as pain. It's all imagination, right?'

'But the pain's horrible, Mr Quimby. Look how red it's become. Oh, oh, the pain's terrible.' Edgar stood, listening, fascinated, and they took absolutely no notice of him.

'See now, ma'am,' said Mr Quimby, 'and listen, right? There are two things in the world, right? One of them's matter – like that bread and that cat sitting by the oven and this hat I was wearing when I came in right? That's matter. Pigs and dust and newspapers and pens and knives and pimples and boils and carbuncles and burns on the hand. Matter, right, *right?* And the other thing is mind, that is to say the thought I'm thinking now and the thought you're thinking, right? Well, matter doesn't really exist, did you know that? Well, you know it now, ma'am. When I see a pig or a pen-knife it's only a thought. It's something I think, right? There's nothing out there, that's true of that cat and that oven it's sitting by, it's all in here here *here*, inside the mind. Right, *right?'*

'I suppose you're going to say that this pain is inside too?' cried the baking-woman. 'That this burnt hand is inside the mind?'

'And it is too, ma'am,' said Mr Quimby. 'You think it's

26

hurt and red and swollen. All you have to do now is to think it's *not* hurt and red and swollen. Right? Do that, ma'am.' He looked at a huge turnip watch he took out of his waistcoast pocket and said: 'Starting *now*.'

'But that's nonsense,' Edgar couldn't resist saying. 'I mean, if it was a toothache the tooth would have to come out, wouldn't it? It would still be a bad tooth even if you said it's only in the mind? Right?'

To his amazement, the baking-woman, whose hand really looked terribly red and painful, cried out: 'Spirit is immortal truth and matter is mortal error. Spirit is the real and eternal and matter is the unreal and temporal.'

'That's right, ma'am,' said Mr Quimby. 'You sure are learning fast.'

'Learning?' she said indignantly. 'What do you mean – learning? I've always known it. It's me who am the teacher and you who are the learner. And *you're* going to learn fast. Now.' And she picked up a long bread-knife from the table and lunged at him with it. 'Right?' she said.

'Ow,' cried Mr Quimby as he ran round the table, the knife after him 'ow, ow, that got me in the elbow, ma'am, ow ow ow ow, you've ripped the cloth from the back of my portland jacket, ow, that was right in the main artery, ma'am.'

'All in the mind,' she cried.

Edgar got away very quickly, as he did not like either the big bread-knife or the look in the baker-woman's eye. So, hearing the cries of Mr Quimby and the shouts of 'All in the mind, right, *right?*' he walked on and on, and soon began to feel very thirsty. The sun was hot and he had nothing to drink since lunchtime. A seagull flew up to him and, hovering in front of his eyes, scrawked: 'All in the mind, eh, sonny? Hahahaha.' Then it flew off.

It was not long before Edgar came to a lane to his left, full of shady trees, and, as he walked under them, grateful for the coolness, he saw a kind of arch woven out of what seemed to be paper leaves and flowers and the sign EDEN in electric lights that were, surprisingly, since it was a bright summer afternoon, flashing feebly in and out like an advertisement for car-tyres or chewing gum. Some bulbs did not, however seem to be working. He walked under the arch and there saw a cheerful little man picking himself up out of a huge pool of mud. The road ahead was all full of such pools, as if there had been very heavy rain quite recently, though there had been no such signs on the esplanade from which Edgar had just turned off. The little man, desperately covered in mud, spoke in a friendly and cheerful manner, shaking mud out of his ears, pouring out of a battered top hat which he then put back jauntily on his head not only mud but also frogs that croaked cheerfully.

'It's all in the mind,' said the man. 'Cheerful within means cheerful without, and don't' – laughing heartily – 'ask me without what.'

'Eden,' said Edgar. 'Eden's another name for paradise, isn't it?'

'All in the mind,' said the man. Coming towards Edgar he suddenly slipped and went down into another mud-bath, from which he emerged as cheerful as before, if not more so. 'You'll get to like it if you keep cheerful. And there's no charge to go in. You don't have to give me not a penny, not a hiddekel (or tigris, if that's the name you prefer) not a euphrates or a pison or a gihon. In you go, and remember it's all, ha ha ha ha, in the mind.' Edgar thanked him and walked on, hearing the little man fall into yet another pool and chuckling heartily, but not, since he was now behind him, seeing him.

Edgar had never in his whole life seen so miserable a

place. The sun was not shining; the sky was covered with rain-clouds, and there was a horrible smell of glue-factories. The houses he saw were black with soot and out of the chimneys of the big black buildings came black smoke that made him cough. There was a big banner stretching across the street, and it said: EDEN MEANS DELIGHT, AND DON'T FORGET IT. There were a lot of big black flies buzzing fretfully around, and Edgar said to himself: 'Whether it's all in the mind or not, I'll be glad when I can find someone to tell me where I have to go in order to get back to school and then home to tea.' There now appeared a very strange-looking lady, riding a white horse, wearing clothes of an earlier age, including a huge hat with a muslin veil (to keep off the flies, Edgar thought), and she carried a whip. With this whip she kept beating at a small Indian in a turban but not much else. He was running ahead of her, and, though he cried repeatedly: 'Oh, you stop that now, *missi-sahib*, oh my goodness, that is very provoking, indeed, on my word, yes, *missi-sahib*, you stop it now, please,' he did not seem to be hurt. Indeed, the whip never seemed to reach him. But the lady kept calling: '*Jildi*, *hitheroa*, I'll tan your hide, by the Lord Harry, I'll thrash you within an inch of your life,' and she lifted up her whip, that whistled through the air, again. The turbaned Indian, catching sight of Edgar, ran behind him for protection, saying: 'She becoming very angry, oh my goodness, yes, but you are my father and mother, *sahib*, and you will keep off her anger from me, oh on my word, yes.' The lady said:

'Who are you, boy? What are you doing here?'

'I'm trying to get back home for tea.'

'Tea,' she said musingly, 'tea. Never touch it myself, bad for the liver, much prefer a whisky *pawnee*, a *chota peg*, do you understand? If you really like tea, and there are some who do, do you understand, you'll have to go up country for it, ah yes.'

29

'You speak true, *missi-sahib*', said the Indian from behind Edgar. 'Up country very good tea.'

'Well, he should know,' she said. 'Born here, drinks it himself. why was I beating the blue living daylights out of him? Can't think why for the moment. Must be a reason, though, do you understand?'

'Very good exercise for you, *missi-sahib*, ha ha. And for me too, goodness gracious, yes.'

'You see up there,' said the lady, pointing with her whip. 'That semi-detached house on the hill. Dreadful place, of course – only fit for a semi-attached couple – what, what?' She roared with laughter, the Indian joined in, going:

'Oh, very funny, *missi-sahib*, you very funny lady, oh my goodness yes. Ha ha ha.'

'Anyway,' said the lady, 'you go up there, boy, and ask. And now', she said to the Indian, 'as for you, you lump of lazarooshian leather you, I'm going to curry you and flay you, do you understand?'

'Aha, you very funny, *missi-sahib*.' And then: 'Ow, ow, you not do that, oh my goodness, please not,' as he ran ahead, though the whip always kept missing him.

Edgar obeyed her instruction, and climbed up a little hill at the top of which were two houses attached to each other – which raised the question of which door to knock at. Edgar chose the first one he came to at the top of the winding path up the hill. At once, to his terror, a very large snake opened it, apparently using its tail to manage the door handle. 'Yes?' it hissed. It wore an old-fashioned lady's bonnet. Edgar, trembling, wondered if this was the mother of the Blatant Beast, or perhaps the Blatant Beast itself. 'Yes? Yessssss?' it hissed again. 'Don't wasssssste time, boy. Have you never sssseen a sssssnake before?'

'Sorry, ma'am,' trembled Edgar. 'I was told that if I came

He went to the house next door and banged there, and this time a rather pleasant-looking old gentleman opened up, dressed rather in the style of Shakespeare . . .

31

here I would be told the way back to school and then home to tea, so I was told anyway.'

'All those tolds,' said the snake crossly. 'I know nothing about schools, boy. I never went to school. I didn't need to. I knew everything when I was born. And now I know more than everything, being older now than I was then.'

'Is it possible to know more than everything, ma'am?' Edgar asked boldly but politely.

'If it's possible to know less than nothing,' said the snake, frowning. 'And I should imagine you know less than nothing about, let me see, let me see, ah yes, about the gentleman who lives next door.'

'That's true, ma'am,' Edgar said, 'if nothing means the same as less than nothing.'

'No, it does not mean the sssssame,' and the snake hissed angrily. 'Because, if you've been to school at all (and why aren't you at school now is what I could ask but won't), you'd know that minus one is less than nothing. And now, since we're on to numbers, give me the biggest number there is, because that would be about the same as everything.'

'It would take too long,' Edgar said. 'When I was a very little boy I took a big exercise book to bed with me on a summer's evening, and I tried to write the last number of all. But I couldn't do it.'

'Of course you couldn't,' snapped the snake. 'Because even if you filled a million billion trillion quadrillion quintillion sextillion septillion octillion nonillion exercise books, you'd still be able to go on adding another digit. And I,' said the snake, 'I I I would be able to add one more. And one more. And one more. So, you see, I know more than everything. Good afternoon.' And she slammed the door shut with her head.

Edgar was not convinced by her argument, but he did not

feel like banging on the door again to reopen it (the argument, that was, but it would also, of course, have meant the door as well), since he did not like the bad-tempered hissing and was a little put out by the idea of a big snake wearing a lady's bonnet and living in a house. What did it, or she, live *on*? He shuddered to think. He went to the house next door and banged there, and this time a rather pleasant-looking old gentleman opened up, dressed rather in the style of Shakespeare – doublet and hose and ruff – who said, smiling:

'Yes?'

'I was told to come here, sir,' Edgar said, 'to ask you how I can find my way home.'

'Come in, come in,' cried the old man, and he led the way along a dusty corridor full of maps and globes. 'I know all about getting to places.' Edgar followed him into a big room, just as dusty as the corridor, which, like the corridor, was full of maps and globes. 'It is my mission, so to speak, in life, so to say, and I'll soon, so to put it, put you right. I suppose,' he said, 'you've been next door?' He laughed loudly. 'They all go next door first, so to speak, and quite a shock it must be to meet Miss Lilith, as she calls herself. Eden Bower she calls her little house, a pretty name. I, for my part, so to express it, am called Richard Eden.'

'Is everything and everybody called Eden, then?' Edgar asked. 'Oh, my name is Edgar.'

'Edgar Edgar Edgar,' said the old man. 'Oh yes,' he said, 'so to say, everything is a bit edenified round here. Hence the name, you know, so to speak.' Then he began to fuss about among his ancient dusty maps, all of which looked to Edgar far too old to be of any use today, since they were all full of blank spaces called TERRA INCOGNITA, meaning *unknown land*, and this was true of a map of England even, which was all blank just north of London. There was a map of America on which it

33

said HERE BE DRAGONS in the populous state of New Jersey.

'I want to get back to school and then home to tea,' Edgar said, looking for somewhere to sit down but finding only maps and globes, also still feeling very thirsty. Tea tea tea, he kept thinking. A nice cup of tea with milk and sugar. And some sweet biscuits. And a few buns. And thin bread and butter. And a pot of cherry jam.

'I should imagine you must be, so to speak, very thirsty. Perhaps very hungry also, so to express it,' said Mr Eden.

'I'd give anything, sir,' Edgar said. 'I'd even give more than anything' (thinking of the snake, Miss Lilith) 'for a nice cup of tea.'

'Tea?' almost screamed Mr Eden. 'Oh, you can't have tea. Far too expensive. Why, there can't be more than a half-ounce in the whole country, so to put it, and I should imagine that Her Majesty the Queen, may she live for ever, so to speak, has gotten hold of it. Eats it she does, mixed with a little salt, so to express it, and nobody is allowed to tell her that that's not the way.' He shook his head sadly and humorously and then let out a great shout, swivelling round to a square-shaped hole in the wall, about the size of a rather small picture. 'Maria!' he yelled. 'Maria, Maria, to express it briefly and sharply and punctiliously!' Then he winked at Edgar.

'Yes, sorr, yer honour,' came a little voice from the hole. 'What is it you'd be wanting at all at all, and me in the middle of me castle rackrent?'

'Fancies herself, you know, so to speak,' said Mr Eden. 'Been to America as a pioneer, as she termed it, and met up with Edgar Huntly.' He looked very closely at Edgar and said: 'You're not the gentleman by any chance now, are you? No, no, you're too young, so to express it, and you haven't pion ears. Well, it stands to reason she couldn't have been where she says she's been – California and the Wild West and so on – because those aren't marked on the map yet. See, so to speak.' And, indeed, beyond a bit of the north-east coast, there wasn't much of America on any of his maps.

'Maria!' called Mr Eden again. 'Fetch something to eat and drink for this young gentleman here, so to speak.'

'Oh sorr,' returned the voice, 'I'm right in the middle of me Frank and me Harry and Lucy. But I'll come right enough and I'll bring what's fitting to be brought for the likes of him, whoever he happens to be, bless us and save us.'

'Good, so to utter it,' called Mr Eden. 'Now then, I think your best way home, which, so to word it accurately, is your immediate and ultimate concern, is to go by way of Newfoundland and the West Indies. Yes yes yes.' And, totally absorbed, he began to measure distances on a big globe with a dusty pair of protactors. While he was doing this a very large mouse came out of the hole in the wall, saying:

'Ah sorr, the pity of it, but there's nothing in the house at all at all but maps and globes, which is well and good for a nibble for the likes of us, sorr, but not what would be giving the nourishment as a young spalpeen like himself now would be requiring at all at all.' The mouse had very busy whiskers and a little skirt on.

'Oh well then,' Mr Eden said, 'I can't oblige you so to speak except with a song, but perhaps a song will cure the thirst, so to put it, and Maria here will join in the chorus.'

'But I'm in the middle of me moral tales and me belindas, sorr,' said the mouse, in a voice that was not at all squeaky.

'You do as I say, Maria,' said Mr Eden in a gruff voice, 'and don't be giving yourself airs, so to speak, about your pioneering days in places that don't exist yet.' And then under his breath he muttered: 'Edgar Huntly, indeed, so to speak.'

35

Then he raised his voice, which was already very high and
wavery, and sang this song:

> *'You can drink the waters of all of the seas*
> *If you take out the saltiness first,*
> *For salt's very good with a piece of cheese*
> *Or to season celery, beans and peas,*
> *And anything else that your palate may please,*
> *But it will not slake your thirst.'*

There was a silence then, and Mr Eden said: 'Come on,
Maria, join in the chorus,' but the mouse said:

'Ah, sure now, sorr, me heart gets near to breaking when I
think of cheese.'

'Never mind about the cheese. The chorus, Maria, so to
speak.'

Then they both sang:

> *'Salt is nice to melt the ice*
> *But it will not melt your thirst.'*

Mr Eden sang again solo:

> *'I have drunk of the waters of all the seas,*
> *Till my stomach was fit to burst.*
> *I've been to the north where the oceans freeze*
> *And the south where the porpoise sits at his ease*
> *And the east where the spice-trees bless the breeze,*
> *But I've always found (and believe me, please)*
> *That it will not slake your thirst.'*

Then the chorus, while Edgar grew thirstier and
thirstier:

> *'Salt is the thing of which I sing,*
> *And it will not cure your thirst.'*

Both Mr Eden and the mouse Maria seemed to expect
applause, so Edgar gave it to them. Whereupon Mr Eden bowed
in a very old-fashioned way and said: 'I think Edenborough is
the place for him, don't you, Maria?'

Edgar who was now down on the road, said to a very small soldier, who was coughing bitterly with the dust that was being raised: 'What's he done then?' 'Moi,' *said the soldier,* 'je ne parle pas français.'

'Oh sure now, sorr, and ye took the words straight out of me mouth. That's the place for him now, to be sure it is, don't be talking.'

'And how do I get there, sir?' asked Edgar.

Mr Eden seemed rather embarrassed at that. He said: 'Well, I've not been there myself, of course, so to express myself, not having the time with all the work here, so to speak, and to tell you the truth I can't find it on any of the maps. But Maria here says it exists, so to put it.'

'Oh sure, sorr, it does, and 'tis as foine a place as ever stood upon two legs.'

'Four legs you said, so to speak,' frowned Mr Eden.

'Two and four – sure they're the same thing,' said Maria.

'Ah, no, they're not, as I've repeatedly told you, so to say,' said Mr Eden, growing darker.

'Well now, sorr, that all depends which way you look at it.'

'Oh no, it doesn't, if I may so express it.'

'You'll forgive the observation, sorr, but it does.'

Edgar could see that a boring argument was about to begin, so he took his leave, bowing politely first to both man and mouse and saying 'I am very grateful for all your help' – words which were ignored. Mr Eden and his maid were now throwing dusty maps at each other, and Maria, despite her comparative smallness, was doing very well. The room was full of dust.

Edgar climbed down the hill and saw, in a cloud of outdoor dust this time, a man on a horse in fine armour, a kingly crown on his head, leading a little army that was coughing with the dust. '*Avant, mes amis*,' cried the man on horseback, whom Edgar took to be a French king. '*Moi*, Henry the Fourth of France, am going to fight *lui*, Louis the Fourteenth of France. How dare he do what he's done. *Avant, a la victoire*.' Edgar, who was now down on the road, said to a very small soldier, who was coughing bitterly with the dust that was being raised:

'What's he done then?'

'*Moi*,' said the soldier, '*je ne parle pas français.*'

'But it was English I spoke,' Edgar said.

'Oh, so it was,' laugh-coughed the little soldier. 'I get so mixed up these days, what with fighting for the Germans one day and the Belgians the next, and the Spaniards, as it might be, over the week-end, that I don't know where I am. What was it you said?'

'What's the war all about?'

'*Ich verstehe kein deutsch.*'

'But it was English I was speaking.'

'So it was, so it was. Well, it doesn't do to know what a war's all about, for you might not be inclined to fight it, and if you don't fight wars, where's your bread and butter going to come from, eh? Not to mention a nice pint mug full of very milky tea with sugar in it.'

'I'd give anything for that,' said Edgar.

'I'm sure you would,' said the soldier, 'but where we're going it will most likely be wine.'

'Stop talking in the ranks there!' A sergeant with a great bristling moustache, his uniform all covered in dust, began pushing at the small soldier and then pushing at Edgar. 'You, boy, where's your drum? You should be out at the front there, just a few paces ahead of His Sacred Majesty's steed, beating away for dear life and keeping the men in step.'

'But I'm not in your army,' Edgar said. 'And I'll thank you not to push at me like that.'

'Shall I push you some other way, then?' barked the sergeant. 'Because I can, boy, oh yes, I can. Go on, then – out of it, if you've no stomach for fighting a just war. Sing,' he then cried. 'Sing, you underbred lumps of bone-idolatry, and keep

39

your cowardly hearts up.' At once all the soldiers began to sing, His Sacred Majesty included, though some coughed too much with the dust to make a really musical effort of it all:

'Liberty of conscience,
That's we require:
No banging us with truncheons
And roasting on the fire.
We'll go to church when we wish
Or not, if we desire,
And Friday's not for fish
But steak fried on the fire.'

Edgar watched them march out of sight in a vast cloud of dust, and he himself took the road in the opposite direction, for he felt sure that they could not be marching to Edenborough. Edenborough, he was sure, was not ruled over by King Louis the Fourteenth of France. He was fairly sure, anyway.

CHAPTER III

The Road
to Edenborough

IT WAS a long long walk to Edenborough and Edgar saw very little to admire on the way. On one side were fields with cows in them, and on the other was a stream, parallel to the road, which was full of jumping fish. The cows had been taught to sing. Edgar wondered who had bothered to waste so much time in teaching them, especially as their songs were not very melodious. Their chief song was one that is called *My country 'tis of thee* if you are American and *God save the Queen* (or *King*), if there happens to be a king on the throne – where we have, as I tell Edgar's story, a Queen – God bless her – radiant in beauty and brilliant in brain: Her Majesty – God bless her and save her – Edith the First, with – may she live for ever – a neck so long and white – heaven preserve it – that she is called sometimes – in total and seemly and loyal reverence – Edith Swan Neck) if you happen to be British. The cows could not, of course, manage the words of either version, but they dealt with the tune by each taking one note only. So one cow would bellow the first note, then repeat it (the first and second notes being the same), then there would be a long pause while another cow slowly came to the realisation that it was its turn to sing, and then it would bellow out the third note. It

41

would thus take about three minutes to cover 'My coun tree' (or 'God save our'), and this made the whole procedure very boring. But it gave the cows something to do besides munch grass and make milk, so perhaps it was not all really a waste of time. They had, apparently, another song, much more difficult, and this was *Pop goes the weasel.* They made it sound like a funeral march for marchers without legs.

The fish in the stream on Edgar's right were much more lively. They were jumping for flies, all of which they knew by name, but they never succeeded in catching any. They were quite cheerful about it, and Edgar heard them chirping: 'There goes Frank Jeffrey – missed him again' and 'Harry Brougham always gives me the slip' and 'Sid Smith is too quick for me, bless him.' One old fish, whose jumping was rather painful and awkward, as though he had fishy rheumatics, kept grumbling: 'Bring the constable to them. Bash them with a truncheon,' but none of the other fishes took any notice. They were very pretty fish, silvery with gold-spotted heads, and some of them greeted Edgar with courtesy: 'Travelling with legs, I see, on dry land too. Get wise, my boy, to the truth of the matter. It's all in the water.' Edgar waved to them, smiling with a very dry mouth, but soon forgot them, and the cows too, when he came to a little stall by the side of the road which seemed to have bottled drinks for sale.

This stall, which was protected from the sun by a huge rainbow umbrella, had a flag flying from it which announced: 'SLAKE YOUR ARID THROTTLE WITH EDWIN'S BRISK AND BUBBLING BEVERAGES'. When Edgar came up to it, he found the drink-seller himself laid out at length on the counter of his stall, snoring away. He was, Edgar saw with interest, a large spotted dog with trousers of hideous cut, whose long snout twitched irritably in his sleep. Edgar took advantage of this unconsciousness not (heaven forbid!) to steal but to

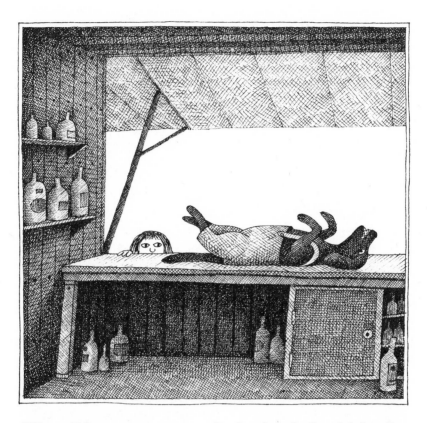

When Edgar came up to it, he found the drink-seller himself laid out at length on the counter of his stall, snoring away. He was, Edgar saw with interest, a large spotted dog with trousers of hideous cut, whose long snout twitched irritably in his sleep.

examine. None of the bottled drinks, which were very cold to the touch despite the hot sun and the lack of ice, were familiar to him. Bishopberry crush, absentee ale, rossettiade, jimandjack juice – he had never met any of them before. He was handling a delightfully chill bottle of Sir Walter Scott's Ineffable And In No Wise To Be Imitated Scotch Soda when he heard a growl: 'Caught you at it, have I, grrrrr?'

'I wasn't stealing, I was looking,' said Edgar. The dog still lay there, frowning and growling, presumably believing that the growl would be enough to frighten Edgar off. 'I'd like to drink something if I may. I'm terribly thirsty.'

'How much money have you got, grrrrr?'

Edgar took out his tiny coin, which he had difficulty in sorting out from the indiarubber and bits of chalk and string and breadcrumbs and ant's eggs in his pocket. 'This,' he said at last. 'One vathek.'

The dog let out a loud laughgrowl: 'Hahahagrrrrrrhahagrrrrahaha. That won't take you very far with me, His Majesty King Edwin, grrrrr. In Northumberland, where I come from, we make very short work grrrrr of folk armed with grrrrr vatheks. So put it down on the counter near my left back paw grrrrr and help yourself to a tiny bottle of Edom O'Gordon's danishberry jumpjuice grrrrr. It has a face on the grrrrr label.' Edgar did as he was told with the coin and then searched for the bottle in question. He had great difficulty in finding it but, at last, from among the shining phalanx of strange drinks, a voice came saying: 'Looking for me, is that it?' Edgar put out his hand, squinting for the source of the voice, while the voice said: 'You're hot, you're hot, now you're cold, now you're very cold, now you're freezing, now you're among the Eskimos, now you're on the North Pole, ah, better, better, ah, now you're on the equator, got me, got me, ah.'

The bottle was indeed a tiny one, and Edgar could hardly see the face on the label, which seemed to be of a jolly man with a black beard – much much smaller than the head of Queen Edith (God bless her) on a doll's house postage stamp. But the voice was fruity and clear. 'Get me down, boy. Go on. Do you the world of good, or bad, depending on how you are.' It seemed a very little portion of drink to cure a thirst, and Edgar did not like the use of the word *bad*. Nevertheless he pulled out the tiny cork between his teeth and promptly swallowed it (it was much too tiny to make him choke). Then he sucked in the tiny drop of drink. It was hard to say what it tasted like but it was as if very very cold ice had been flavoured with currants, raisins, candied peel, chocolate, vanilla, nutmeg and a cut off an over-roasted joint of roast pork. At once Edgar felt a great deal less thirsty. The face on the label became still and silent, but the dog who called himself King Edwin of Northumberland and who had been watching all this time and growling gently to himself, suddenly let out a great bark.

'What's that for?' asked Edgar. 'Did I do something wrong?'

'Bow wow wow,' or something like it, went King Edwin. 'I said you were to help yourself to it, not to drink it.'

'But it means the same thing. If you ask somebody to help himself to a slice of cake, it means eat it. Besides, you didn't tell me to stop when I started drinking.'

'That, bow bow, was to see the badness of you to the limit, which I knew was there. We'd make short work of you in Northumberland, I can tell you. Well now, helping yourself to a piece of cake means eating it, not drinking it. And you drank that stuff up, bow wow, grrrrr.'

'Wrong,' Edgar protested, 'Helping yourself to a book from a shelf doesn't mean eating it, either.'

45

'How do you know, boy, bow wow? In Northumberland where I was a king, they used to *devour* books. I know, because I devoured many myself, grrrrr. But all this is not the point.'

'You mean,' said Edgar, growing annoyed, 'I should have *eaten* that bottle, not drunk it? But that's ridiculous.'

'*I'll* tell you what's ridiculous and what isn't, me being grrrrr King Edwin. Now do what I say, boy, bow grrrrr wow.'

'You mean *eat* the bottle?' shouted Edgar.

'No no no no no, bow wow wow grrrrr. *Read it.*'

Edgar shrugged: this was certainly a *mad* dog. He was just going to say that there was nothing to read on the label except a tiny blackbearded face, but he saw that there was no point in arguing with a mad dog who thought he was King Edwin of Northumberland. So he looked down at the label and, not really to his surprise, found a poem there – written in beautifully clear handwriting and very easy to read. He read it aloud, and the dog gave a kind of purring growl, as though he had cats in his ancestry, which seemed to show that he liked to be read aloud to:

'*Thomas Alva Edison,*
His blood a mix of Scotch and Dutch,
Was dead in 1931,
But he had loved both long and much.
His years of life were 84,
And his inventions manifold,
He knew what telephones were for,
Before the Graham Bell had tolled.
When he was in his 30th year,
Though many folk were prone to laugh,
He startled many a serious ear,
By building the 1st phonograph.
When he had just gone 32,
He showed the true inventive stamp,
By making something brightly new –

46

He was very lucky to be offered a lift by a sort of van that stopped just in front of him in a fog of dust, hooting away on horns that played a little tune. When the dust-fog cleared, Edgar was able to see that written all along the van was the legend THE EDENBOROUGH REVUE.

The electric incandescent lamp.
When photographs had just come hither,
Old T.A.E. went Ha ha ha,
And mad those stillies movies with a
Kinetoscopic camera.'

'An interesting man, that,' said King Edwin, 'grrrrrprrrrr. If we'd had him in Northumberland, there's no knowing what wonders he might have performed. So now then, boy, grrrrr, go on your way to my great city of Edenborough.'

'Yours?' said Edgar.

'Yes, yes, grrrrr yes, they named it after me. It's Edwin-grrrrr, really, though, but they made a mistake when they wrote it down. I didn't correct it, of course, for it was a very cold day, and everybody that came up to me was saying, 'Edwin, brrrrr,' so that was all right.' The dog fell asleep again, snoring loudly, so Edgar, somewhat refreshed, continued his journey.

He still had several miles (or kilometres – more kilometres than miles, of course) to go before he got there. At one point he came to a big notice swinging high over the road, secured to two pillars that woodpeckers were happily pecking away at, which said: 'SEVERAL MILES TO EDENBOROUGH. SEVERAL X 1.609 KILOMETRES TO THE SAME. BUT IT WILL BE WORTH IT!' He was very lucky to be offered a lift by a sort of van that stopped just in front of him in a fog of dust, hooting away on horns that played a little tune. When the dust-fog cleared, Edgar was able to see that written all along the van was the legend THE EDENBOROUGH REVUE. He ran to it, the driver already had the door open, and he entered, saying thank you with real gratitude, to find that the interior part of the van was filled with little men who greeted him cheerfully. When Edgar had found a seat – he had to remove a wooden box labelled *Best Finnan Haddie* and a heavy tabby cat that was

48

guarding it – these little men were very eager to explain who they were and what the Edenborough Revue was. They, they said, *were* the Edenborough Revue. They sang and danced and told jokes and acted sketches, and one of them, who said his name was Tommy Carlyle, did impersonations. He was a sad little man who rolled his r's a great deal and kept saying: 'Aye, aye, och, weel, that's the way o' it.'

'What kind of impersonations?' Edgar wanted to know.

'Och, weel, aye – here's one o' King Edward the First o' England.' (While he was saying that, Edgar thought: oh no, back to all those boring Anglo-Saxon kings, but then he remembered that Edward the First was *not* Anglo-Saxon). Tommy Carlyle composed his sad face into a look of haughty majesty. Then he said: 'And the noo – King Edward the Second.' He made the same face as before. 'And the noo,' he said: ' – King Edward the Third.' It was still the same haughtily majestic face.

Edgar said: 'Is that all you do – the King Edwards of England?'

'Och,' said Tommy Carlyle, 'there's an awful lot o' them. Nine to ma computation.'

'Eight, surely,' said Edgar. 'Edward the Eighth was the last one. He ruled less than a year. Since then it's been – oh, certainly no more Edwards.'

'Och, ye wee sleekit cowerin' beastie,' said Tommy Carlyle. 'There is unco' little ye ken aboot it and that's a fac'. Edward the Ninth – aye, there was a monarch for ye, Sassenach though he was.' And he composed his sad face into a look of haughty majesty. The rest of the troupe clapped vigorously, so Edgar joined in against his will, and Tommy Carlyle made a sad bow.

'Nobody like Tommy,' said a man who called himself Mr Gladstone and nursed a heavy bag on his knee. 'He always brings

49

the house down in Edenborough.'

'What do *you* do, sir?' asked Edgar.

'Play the piano on the black notes, me,' winked Mr Gladstone. 'And old Tom Macaulay over there – he plays the piano on the white notes.'

The man referred to, who was smoking a big pipe that smelt of burning paper, nodded and nodded to show this was true.

'At the same time?' Edgar asked.

'Well, yes,' Mr Gladstone said. 'We get a bit tangled up, of course, sometimes. But if you've got all those black and white keys it stands to reason they all have to be played, otherwise there's no point in paying for them. That's right, Tom, isn't it?'

'Right, Bill, right.' And Mr Macaulay nodded. A piece of burning paper fell from his pipe on to the cat, which took no notice at all as it soon went out (the burning paper, not the cat).

'But it must sound – well, pretty awful,' said Edgar.

Mr Gladstone smiled. 'That's what they all say,' he said. 'Which shows they don't know much about it. Uneducated, that's their trouble. Right, Tom?'

'Right, Bill, right.'

'You have to be brought up to it,' said Mr Gladstone. Then he took a newspaper out of his pocket and began to read the front page with close and frowning attention. The newspaper seemed to be at least a hundred years old. A man who looked nearly as old, and bent and stiff but who said he was a dancer (and that his name was Sir J. Stephen), now said:

'Not read it yet, Bill? You've been on that same page to my certain knowledge for the last fifty-five – no, I'm telling a lie – the last fifty-six point five five five recurring years.' Mr Gladstone said very sternly:

'There's almost more than meets the eye, that's why you

have to read with very close attention. Right, Tom?'

'Right, Bill, right.'

'For instance, it says here: BANK ROBBERS GET AWAY WITH FIFTEEN THOUSAND POUNDS. Now I've been thinking of the true meaning of that for something like –'

'Fifty-six point five five five recurring years,' said Sir J. Stephen.

'Very well. And I think it really means that they got away with fifteen months – that being their prison sentence, you know.'

'You mean,' said Edgar,' that *thousand pounds* is a kind of code for *months*?'

'It could be,' said Mr Gladstone gravely. 'You have to look very deep into it. They always say that time is money. Right, Tom?'

'Right, Bill, right.'

'It would mean,' said Edgar, working it swiftly out in his head, 'five hundred pounds a day in September, April, June and November.'

'Well, there you are then,' said Mr Gladstone in triumph. 'And with twenty-five hours a day – which is what I want, and what I'm determined to get in the next parliament – that would mean – well, you work it out, boy.'

'Twenty pounds an hour,' said Edgar immediately.

'And not bad pay either,' said a man in clown's costume called Art Stanley. 'Better than what *we* get.' Then he looked sternly from his painted face out of the window, and Edgar looked too. There was a view of mountains and a beautiful big lake shining in the sun, and there seemed to be men dancing about on its nearest shore. 'There they are, then,' said Art Stanley. 'We'd better get out to 'em.' The rest of the troupe sighed and nodded. Mr Gladstone said to the driver:

'We'll have to get out, Matthew, and bang them about a

bit.' The driver, a man with pencils and pens behind both ears, nodded sadly and braked the van by the side of the road. Edgar said:

'Who? Why?'

'Poets,' said Mr Macaulay, blowing burning paper from his pipe. 'Could never abide this lot. But you have to creep up on them slowly.'

Edgar sighed and asked no more questions. Instead, he got out with the others, who kept whispering 'Shhhhh' very loudly to each other and began to crawl feebly through the long grass. Tommy Carlyle started to sneeze.

'Shhhhh. SHHHHHHHHHHHH!'

'Ah canna help it, mon. It's the hay feverrr. Arch WHOOOOO!'

There were about a dozen of these men dancing about by the lake, all rather thin and tall except for one, who was fat and panted a lot and said:

'What's the summmmject or ommmmject of the exercise?'

'Listen now,' said a thin man with a mad look and a lot of teeth. 'It's to get the inspiration working. Inspiration means breathing, you see, and now we're all breathing really hard.' Then he began to recite:

> *'A daffodil's a little flower*
> *That gets its money by the hour.*
> *It blues the money, more or less,*
> *And buys itself a yellow dress.*
> *It flounces and is very vain*
> *But does not mind a drop of rain*
> *Or e'en when typhoons tear the County,*
> *Since it is all from Nature's bounty.'*

Tommy Carlyle, lying in the grass trying to control his sneezing, gave out a loud baying sound, like a dog that howls at the moon, and cried: 'Och, the blitherin' blatherskite. Och, the sheer horror o' it.' Mr Gladstone nodded resignedly at the others, and then called:

'Forward the Light Brigade!'

What Edgar saw then was not very edifying. The members of the Edenborough Revue leapt rather feebly on the poets and tried to throw them into the lake. But the fat poet who had talked of summmmjects and ommmmjects raised his hands into the air and said: 'Magic. Poetry is magic. Both the summmmject and the ommmmject.' And he recited, while the thinner poets were being put into the lake and then coming out again to put the Edenborough Revue into it:

> *'A weasel plonked a large guitar*
> *Upon the coast of Barbary*
> *Where all the deadly lemmings are*
> *And wisdom is a foul cigar*
> *Smoked by Sir Hubert Laurelee,*
> *And bayed her blessings to the sun*
> *And croaked a creaking malison*
> *Upon a sole belated star,*
> *And when the dreadful day was done*
> *She dove into the burning sea*
> *And there, for all I know of it,*
> *Her song, suffused with dreadful glee,*
> *May soothe the biter and the bit*
> *And lead the traveller home to tea.'*

Even Edgar, who thought the whole thing was nonsense, was affected by that last line, but the effect on Tommy Carlyle was quite remarkable. 'Och aye,' he said, nodding, 'ma bonny wee laddies, it's no' sae bad, ye ken. Aye, therrre's a cerrrtain quality aboot it, ye maun admit.' The poets took advantage of his momentary admiration to grab hold of him and throw him into the lake, but he still nodded, sitting in the water with fish leaping out of his very loose collar, saying: 'Och aye, there's nae gainsayin' it the noo.' But the rest of the Edenborough Revue troupe grew very angry and began to grab the poets by the hair and throw them in to join Tommy Carlyle. The fat poet was the first to hit the water in this renewed assault, and he lay there crying:

'Now I understand. *His floating hair.* I always wondered what it meant when I wrote it, but now I know.'

Edgar, disgusted by the whole unseemly business, went back to the van, where the driver sat gloomily at the wheel. The cat was sleeping peacefully in the back but it woke rather angrily when Edgar appeared and said, cattily: 'If you've come to steal the finnan haddie you've another think coming, my boyo. I'll scratch you with vigour, also with my claws, so watch out.' Then it went to sleep again and the driver said:

'Always the same. Always always always. I've a good mind to get out of this job altogether and go back to what I was before.'

'And what was that?' asked Edgar politely.

'You see,' the driver said, ignoring the question, 'they've carried that case of finnan haddie about for longer than I can't remember. Now why they don't open it up and eat it is more than what I can't understand. I likes nothing better than some nice poached haddock with a couple of poached eggs on top. But it's my private opinion – and I'd ask you not to noise it abroad overmuch – that they keeps it there just to give the cat something to do. Protect it, you know. Ridiculous.'

'And what was the job you did before?' Edgar asked patiently.

'I used to go round the schools,' sighed the driver. 'Seeing that everybody was teaching proper and that the kids was being taught proper, as you might say. But they wouldn't take no notice of it when I put them right. You'd not hardly credit some

The poets took advantage of his momentary admiration to grab hold of him and throw him into the lake, but he still nodded, sitting in the water with fish leaping out of his very loose collar . . .

of the things the kids was taught.'

'What, for instance?' asked Edgar.

'Well, that William Shakepaw did not write THE DOG OF VENICE, for instance. Nor wrote MUD, SIMMER KNIGHT'S CREAM. Now this Knight's Cream was very good, obtainable from the best of dairies, and it had to be simmered to taste proper, and Mud did it as well as any.'

'What sort of mud?' asked Edgar.

The driver sneered. 'There was only one Mud that I never knew of, he said, 'and that was Albert Mud, a real good cook and the slowest simmerer ever you seen.'

'Look,' Edgar said. 'I think I'll get out and walk, if you don't mind.' For he was really growing very tired of all this stupidity. He would really even have preferred to be yawning in the classroom and hearing about the horrible Anglo-Saxon kings.

'Please yourself,' said the driver huffily. 'It's nearly done, all that flapdoodle out there by the waters. In here they'll be directly, spilling wet over everything. Then we can be on us way. Another thing they said he didn't write was HALL'S WELL THAT END – SWELL. That was a lovely thing. An American gentleman comes to this country looking for Sir Peregrine Hall, that being the man's name. When he gets near where he is they says to him that's Hall's well's over there, and this American gentleman says that's fine and goes over to it.'

'Is that the whole story?' asked Edgar, fascinated despite his disgust.

'Why,' laughed the driver, as though amazed at Edgar's stupidity, 'would you want more? The whole story runs to near twelve hundred pages. There's what happens on the way, see, and what happens afterwards. But if you're like all the others, you'd best get out of my van and make your own way alone.'

'That's right,' said the cat from its sleep. 'I don't care

much for thieves sitting around.'

So Edward got out, just in time to see the Edenborough Revue troupe coming out of the water and the poets dancing about further away than they had been before. The troupe were all very wet, and Edgar did not much like the idea of having to sit with them. So he hurried off down the road, hoping he would reach Edenborough soon. He wanted to get home in time for tea.

CHAPTER IV

Also
the Road
to Edenborough

POOR EDGAR! It was taking him such a long time to get to Edenborough. Poor you too, for that matter: I'm sure your anxiety to get there must be quite as great as his. But if you only knew (and you will know all too soon) what was waiting for Edgar in Edenborough, you would be as happy as I am to put off his arrival there.

What happened to Edgar now was that he was intrigued by some curious-looking blue flowers growing in a cluster by the side of the road (the left side, if you want to know). These flowers seemed to be chattering at a great rate in very high-pitched English, and Edgar had to get very close in order to hear what they were saying. Also, of course, he wished to see where the sounds were coming from, for flowers, although they can sometimes look like faces, have no mouths. The sounds themselves didn't make a great deal of sense to Edgar, and he wondered why flowers should be so excited and talkative about this kind of thing:

'. . . It was King Nidhud told him to do it. He had to put the apple on his own poor son's head and then shoot an arrow at it. Egil – that was his name.'

'You're thinking of William Tell, stupid.'

'Egil. Egil. That was his name. He was the brother of Wayland Smith. You ask Mr Honeythunder. Or Mr Grewgious. They'll tell you all about it.'

Edgar moved closer and closer and then, to his shock and horror, found the ground giving way beneath him. What he had done, of course, was to tread on some grass that covered a deep ditch. Down into this ditch he went: it was a dry ditch, that was one blessing, but it was impossible for him to climb out. The sides of the ditch were of smooth clay, and he could not find a hand-hold anywhere. So he did the only thing he could do, and that was to shout for help. 'Help! Help!' he cried. The flowers did not seem to hear him.

'. . . The question is whether we have free will or it's all worked out ahead for us. You ought to read Jonathan Edwards, missionary to the Red Indians.'

'. . . Boxing is what I like, though we don't see enough of it here. The gentle art of pugilism is what it's called.'

'. . . Egil nothing. It's William Tell you're thinking of. A Swiss he was.'

Edgar was very irritated with the flowers. Luckily he was not hurt, only a little bruised, and the bottom of the ditch was mossy. But he did not want to stay there for ever, so he kept on calling 'Help! Help!'

'. . . You take Philip the Duke of Orleans, for example. Gave himself a new name – Equality, a silly sort of name – but he had his head chopped off just the same.'

'You ought to make a little poem of that. Equality – that was his name. But they cut his loaf off just the same.'

'I said nothing about a loaf, stupid.'

Edgar still went on calling for help and was still ignored by the flowers, but soon he found something heavy sitting on his chest. He could not see very clearly in the dim light of the deep ditch, but he felt sure that it was a big tortoise sitting there. He put up his hand to confirm this, and sure enough there was a great tough shell and a wrinkled lizard head peering from beneath it. The tortoise said:

'Would you like me to go for help?'

'Oh yes please,' Edgar said, but then he reflected that it would take a tortoise a very long time to go for anything. His doubt must have conveyed itself to the tortoise, which now said:

'Think I'll be too slow, is that it? Don't you believe it. From here to Edenborough is less than a mile, and I reckon I could easily be there and back by, say, the Christmas after next. That's not too bad for speed, the way I see it.'

Edgar groaned. He said: 'I don't have all that much time. I'd starve to death, lying here and waiting.'

'Ah, that's because you have a wrong sense of time. You don't live long enough, that's your trouble. Now we tortoises think nothing of living a hundred years. Like parrots, you know. Not that I think much of parrots. They can't really talk, they just imitate. *Pretty Polly* and all that nonsense. *Scratch Polly's head arrrrrrrgh*. Ridiculous.'

'Well,' Edgar sighed, 'if you're going for help perhaps you'd better go now.'

'No need to take that attitude. Plenty of a time for a bit of a chat and a few reminiscences of a long long life. Did I ever tell you about the second King of Rome – Numa his name was? His wife was a kind of a fountain called Egeria.'

'No,' Edgar said patiently, 'you never told me. We haven't met before. And I really do look forward to your telling me, but not now. Please, not now. What I want is to get out of here.'

Before the tortoise could say something offended in reply,

'Give me your hands,' said Crossjay to Edgar. 'Old Durdles has got hold of my ankles.' And so Edgar was yanked up. He was very glad to see the light of day again and feel the road under his feet.

Edgar to his joy heard human voices up there on the road. A lady spoke first:

'Oh, Willoughby, Willoughby, how clever those flowers are. Listen to them talking away.' Then a bored and haughty man's voice replied:

'Fiddlesticks, my dear Laetitia. What they're saying is hardly worth listening to. Not a single original thought in a cart-load of fallen petals.'

'Help! Help!' called Edgar. 'I've fallen into the ditch.'

'Now that,' said the man's voice, 'is just lying stupidity. Flowers don't fall into ditches. Or if they do they don't raise a big noise about it. It's a common hazard of flowers, I should say, to fall into ditches.'

The tortoise said: 'A fat lot he knows about anything,' and the lady said: 'Oh, dear Willoughby, you're *so* right.'

'I'm never wrong, my dear Laetitia,' replied the man, and Edgar called: 'Help! Help! It's a boy that's fallen in. My name is Edgar. Help, please help!'

'Ah,' came the man's voice, 'a boy, eh? I don't care much for boys. Not reverent enough. No appreciation of their betters. Best let him stew in his own juice.'

'Oh, Willoughby, no! That would be too cruel!'

'Think so, eh? Very well. Let's have young Crossjay over here.' And he called: 'Crossjay, let us be having you.' Then he said: 'What I said was hardly apposite, my dear Laetitia. Stew in his own juice no, one can hardly say that. Rot in his own ditch – that's better, eh, eh?'

But now Edgar saw a jolly young round face peering down at him. This was Crossjay, Edgar supposed. 'Ah,' smiled Crossjay, as Edgar supposed him to be, 'got a tortoise on you. That's good, that's very good. Fond of tortoises I am meself. What's your name, old fellow?'

'Edgar,' Edgar replied.

'No, no, I meant the tortoise. Oh, offended, is it?' For the tortoise was now crawling away. It said to Edgar:

'Can't stand familiarity. I'm old enough to be that boy's great great grandfather. Well, I'll see you sometime, I suppose. Glad to have been of service.' And off it went.

'Give me your hands,' said Crossjay to Edgar. 'Old Durdles has got hold of my ankles.' And so Edgar was yanked up. He was very glad to see the light of day again and feel the road under his feet. The man called Durdles was very old and bald and seemed to be covered with stone-dust. He said to Edgar:

'Everyone to his taste, I suppose. But if it's lying in earth you wish to be, I have some very nice graves new-dug over in the churchyard, and I'll do you a lovely headstone for next to nothing. With cherubs on it too.'

The lady called Laetitia was tall and thin, but the man called Willoughby was even thinner and taller and he had what looked like a perpetual sneer on his face. 'Before we go any further,' he said haughtily to Edgar, 'I would have you know that I am to be addressed as *Sir* Willoughby.' He had a very tall grey hat on.

'Well,' Edgar said, 'grateful as I am for your help, I don't think the occasion for my calling you anything is likely to be much prolonged. For I must hurry on to Edenborough. Let me then reiterate my gratitude and take my leave.'

'Oh,' said Laetitia, 'he speaks so like a gentleman. You must try your poem out on him, Willoughby.' And it seemed to Edgar that she was rather proud of not having to call him *Sir* Willoughby. That she was not his wife Edgar had no doubt. Her clothes were very poor and full of mended tears, whereas he was dressed like a dandy. Sir Willoughby said, in a bored voice:

'Oh, very well. It is up to the already enlightened to

spread the light, I suppose. Eh? I think that's rather good, eh, eh, what?' All this time Crossjay was peeling an apple he had taken from his pocket, using a very blunt knife and grumbling softly in a good-humoured way. 'Here it is, then,' said Sir Willoughby, and he struck a dignified posture like an actor:

'I used to know two Eliots,
Both good with words and stops and commas.
They started writing in their cots:
The first was George, the other Thomas.
Now one of them, despite the name,
A woman was, and not a man.
But which was which? – A crying shame,
I do not know. For though I can
Distinguish between types of wine
And playing-cards (all fifty-two)
And weather foul and weather fine
And faces in a boat-race crew,
Orang-utan and marmoset
And cherry pie and apple tart,
Alas alack I never yet
Could tell the Eliots apart.'

Before the lady called Laetitia could clap her hands and say how wonderful it was or Edgar could murmur something politely admiring, Sir Willoughby held up his right hand sternly and said:

'You must understand that I really do know which was which, but the sensible thing to do now and then is to pretend not to know everything. Otherwise people regard one as uppish. Hence,' he said, 'the poem.'

'Too many words,' grumbled Durdles. 'It'd be hard work getting all them words carved on a gravestone. Still, everyone to his taste, I suppose.'

'The point is,' repeated Sir Willoughby, 'that I really do know which was which. All that was poetic licence.'

'Done it at last!' cried little Crossjay, holding up his peeled apple. 'Thought as how I should never get it done. Oh, well.' And he threw the apple away into the long grass. He smiled at Edgar and said: 'Can't stand the taste of 'em. It's the peeling of 'em I really like.'

'Again thank you,' Edgar said. 'And now I really must be on my way.' And he bowed in a very old-fashioned and courtly manner, so that Laetitia giggled and said:

'Such a polite little boy.'

'I know which is which,' said Sir Willoughby loudly and crossly.

'So,' said Edgar, 'good day to one and all.'

'I've a little grave just right for you,' said Durdles. 'Won't be at all right for you in six months time, boys growing the way they do, but now it would be fine. Come and see it.'

'I know, I do really know!'

'Of course you do, Willoughby dear.'

'Won't take a minute to view it,' Durdles said. Edgar began to run. He ran and ran until he turned a corner. He could still hear Sir Willoughby shouting crossly:

'I know, I know, I really do know!'

But soon he could hear nothing more, and all his attention was taken up by the sight of the great city of Edenborough, which stretched below him in the late afternoon sunlight. He stood on a hill, and down there was a fine wooded valley with a silver river running through it like a monstrous snake, and on the river, which had many bridges, stood the city with its shining domes. 'Edenborough,' breathed Edgar to himself, and a little voice near him repeated the name in tones of disgust. 'Edenborough,' it said. 'Pah!' Edgar looked down to see a little grey man dressed

65

all in grey, leaning on a crooked stick. 'And what,' said the little man frowning, 'might your name be, if, as seems more likely than not, you have such? Come on, answer.'

'Edgar, and what's yours?'

'I'll give you three guesses,' said the little man. Edgar needed only one. He said:

'Grey?'

'Depends on how you spell it. If you spell it with an *e*, no. With an *a*, yes. Gray.'

'You seem,' said Edgar, 'to have a very low opinion of that great city spread all before us in the valley.'

'And so I have,' said Mr Gray. 'I wrote a poem about it once. Listen.'

Nearly everybody Edgar had met this day seemed to have a poem to recite; nevertheless, he hid his sigh and politely lent an ear. The little man recited, bitterly:

> '*On well-heeled feet and tartan-trousered legs,*
> *They jeer and leer and sneer at all who come.*
> *They sift soft sugar over hard-boiled eggs,*
> *They chew the crust and throw away the crumb.*
>
> *They season herrings with vanilla custard,*
> *And groaningly they grind at ground-up gristle,*
> *They sup cold soup because they say they must. A d-*
> *-ay goes hardly by without they whistle.*'

Very difficult,' said Mr Gray, 'to find a rhyme for *custard*. Now here comes the important bit. Listen carefully –

> '*They hear loud music every time they feast,*
> *They play a sort of game with bat and ball.*
> *They feed their children to the Blatant Beast*
> *And to his dam, and do not care at all.*'

'What is all that about a beast and a dam?' said Edgar, who could not hear very clearly, since Mr Gray had recited this last verse in a mumbling undertone.

'Dam? His mother, of course,' said Mr Gray. 'But you'll see soon enough. Now don't interrupt. I'm coming to the last verse, and this sums it all up. Listen –

> *'An old man's curse cast spavin on their hocks.*
> *Soon they'll be glad to go into the dark.*
> *I'll find for each a cast-iron wooden box*
> *And feed them to the turkeys in the park.'*

He nodded direly and said: 'I don't think that's going too far at all. You'll see when you get there.' Then he hobbled off away from the town, leaning on his stick and muttering. Edgar, with joy and hope in his heart, made his way down the hill towards Edenborough. That poem was all a lot of nonsense.

CHAPTER V

E and D
and G and A

A H, EDENBOROUGH – so delightful a town it seemed. Edgar walked with pleasure through its comely streets, but all the time he was looking for a way back to the classroom and then home to tea (surely by now the lesson must be over). He asked many of the charming policemen he saw smilingly patrolling the tree-clad avenues and shining shopping thoroughfares: 'How shall I get back?' And they nearly all said.

'Wait till four o'clock, sonny.'

The town seemed to be full not only of native Edenborough folk but of people from distant countries like Brazil, Jamaica, Honduras, South Africa, Red China, Blue China and White China. Tourists, said Edgar to himself. They all had guidebooks and cameras, and they leafed away and clicked away, for there was much to see and read about and record. These were some of the things:

The Boxing Museum with Living Specimens of Ancient and Modern Pugilism.

The Mechanical Statue of Pierce Egan, Author of Over Twenty Thousand Pieces of Cheap Literature.

A working Model of Egdon Heath.

The Eglinton Tournament with Jousting Knights and Firespitting Fiery Steeds, Together with Lovely Ladies Cheering them on.

Egyptian Thieves in Safe Cages.

Eidothea, Daughter of the Master of a Million and One Disguises.

An Eisteddfod of Bards, Singing and Reciting in Genuine Welsh.

El Dorado, the City of Gold, in Miniature but Complete in Every Detail, Complete with the Gold King, also in Miniature, its Ruler.

Domenico Theotocopuli, Painting Visitors on the Spot in Bright Colours and With Distorted Shapes, but Very Cheap and Remarkably Quickly Done.

The Roman Emperor Heliogabalus Raging and Screaming.

Elaine le Blank, A Pretty Girl but Not Very Bright. Rather Silly In Fact.

Electra and Her Ten Thousand Coloured Electric Lamps.

The Elephant in the Moon.

Genuine Elves in Little Green Coats, Stealers of Children and Causes of Nightmares, But All Safely Locked Up and Unable to Do Any Harm at All, Ha Ha.

The Play of Elijah in Four Scenes: (i) He is Given a Meal by Ravens at the Brook Called Kerith (ii) He raises the Dead Son of the Widow of Zarephath (iii) He Confutes the Prophets of Baal (iv) He Is Carried Up to Heaven in a Chariot of Fire.

Elisha Being Mocked at by Children Who are at once Most Cruelly Though Quite Justly Really Destroyed by Big Brown and Black Bears. A Musical Play with New and Original Songs and Dances.

Elizabeth and Her German Garden.

St Elmo's Fire, This Being the Ball of Light Commonly Seen on the Masts and Yard Arms of Ships During Storms at Sea. Also Called Corposant.

An Hourly Lecture by Ralph Waldo Emerson, a Very Learned and Most Interesting American Gentleman All the Way from Boston Mass.

The Story of the Witch of Endor, Very Frightening, Told by Sir Endymion Latmos.

ENGLAND EXPECTS THAT EVERY MAN WILL DO HIS DUTY, famous signal of Lord Nelson at the Battle of Trafalgar: six easy lessons on how to convey *This Important Message* with Flags, Flags, And More Flags.

The Lady Quintessence Will Allow Her Hand to Be Kissed in Her Castle, Ever Open (at a Price) To Visitors, called Entelechy.

Etc Etc Etc Etc Etc.

There was a great clock high up above the main street of the city and at four o'clock on the dot it began to strike and then play a charming tune which to Edgar sounded like *Pop goes the weasel* upside down. And when the tune had jangled to stillness, Edgar was interested to see crowds of people making their way to what signposts called Walkinshaw Square. Some, he saw with curiosity, were unwilling to go there, but the smiling charming police herded them along, making the sort of noise that horsemen make to horses. Edgar politely approached a big fat police sergeant, all blue and silver and gold, and said:

'How do I get back?'

'You get back by going forward,' said the policeman. 'Go with this lot to the square there. Listen carefully. Can you hear the band playing? You go there and everything will be as right as ninepence.' He smiled in a friendly way, then he pushed Edgar rather rudely and roughly into the moving crowd. A man next to him said:

'Making you go there too, are they? Well, all I can say is that I'd rather be old and tough as I am and not young and tender like what you are. But it all depends, after all, on the tune that they play, don't it?'

'I don't know,' Edgar said. 'I've never been here before.'

'And you'll not be here again, if you've half a centimetre of sense in that young noddle of yours,' said a fat wheezing old woman.

Then Edgar thought of Mr Gray and his poem and a shiver went down his spine. There was something not quite right about Edenborough. There was something quite certainly wrong about some of the signs above the shops: T. MOORE'S CHOCOLATE CLOCKS AND WATCHES – THE EPIGO SHOP FOR ACHES AND CHILLS – CURE THAT COUGH WITH ENTENT CORDIAL–EPIDAURUS'S LIVE SUGAR MICE. He said to the man next to him:

'What are they going to do to us?'

'You'll see. It's all for the tourist trade. Tourists coming here spending money. Disgraceful, I call it.'

'Don't you want their money, then?' asked Edgar.

'Money isn't everything,' said the man. 'What I like best in all the world to eat is a nice roast diadoch.'

'A what?'

'Diadoch, diadoch, have you never heard of a diadoch? Now you can't buy one of these with all the money in the world. So what good is their dirty money is what I say. Ah, here we are then.'

The square was crowded. There were buildings all round it, all with names on them – LITTLE ERIC; HANKY AND PANKY; ER; ERNEST MALTRAVERS; A. E. OEXME-LIN; ESTHER WATERS (BOTH PLAIN AND MINERAL) – and from the windows many people looked out (tourists?)

clicking cameras in the sun. In the centre of the square, which was shaped like a circle, there was a fine big statue of a man on horseback, and this statue seemed to be conversing, with many shakes and nods of his metal head, to a man in clown's costume (was he a member of the Edenborough Revue troupe?). There was a big band up on a bandstand, conducted by an immensely tall and thin man in military uniform and gloves of dazzling white, and the band was at the moment playing something soft and rather dreamy. Then, without warning, it went into a very fierce loud chord, with cymbals clashing, and the clown leapt into the air several times. Then he ran, with much comic tripping, to a bank of microphones, all with names – TUC, TOP, HOW, UPP, YOU, QZXERVK – and cried, his voice booming from loudspeakers all over the square:

'You all know why we're here this gorgeous sprinter, or is it smautumn, afterlunch, and we'll waste no more time, shall we not, no we shan't, not by no manner of means shall we not, my friends, and also my mother-in-law who I see down there, yoo hoo. So on with it.' He made a big conducting gesture at the conductor, who made a big conducting gesture at the band, and then the whole band played just one note. This one:

A very old lady just in front of Edgar said: 'What was it? I didn't hear it, deaf as a post I am.' And many people said: 'E. E. That's what it is, E. The note E.'

'Oh, that's all right,' she said. 'My name's Doreen, so I don't have to stay.' And off she went, and many others went with her. Edgar didn't understand. He said to a small fat man who was chewing what looked like long black bootlaces:

In the centre of the square, which was shaped like a circle, there was a fine big statue of a man on horseback, and this statue seemed to be conversing, with many shakes and nods of his metal head, to a man in clown's costume (was he a member of the Edenborough Revue troupe?).

'I just don't understand.'

'Simple enough,' said this man, chewing. 'Those whose names don't begin with an E just goes. Just goes. Me, I'm of the name of Edward, so I stays. Listen.' For the band had started to play again. It gave out two notes this time:

'And that means I stays,' said the man. 'An E and a D, and me being of the name of Edward. What's your name then, sonny?' Edgar told him. 'Why then, you stays too.' And now the band gave out three notes. The square was emptying fast, and those who were leaving were smiling with relief. The three notes were:

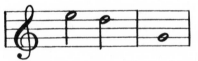

'An E and a D and a G,' said the chewing man. 'Well, that lets me out, me being of the name of Edward, which is an E and a D and a W. What did you say your name was, then?' Edgar told him again. 'Well, then that's an E and a D and a G, like what they just played. Good-bye and the very best of luck.' And he went, the bootlaces he was chewing (probably liquorice) hanging from his mouth and waving in the wind. By now the square was almost empty, but the tourists were still clicking away with their cameras. Edgar called to a young man standing about a hundred yards from him:

'What is your name, sir?'

'Me?' said the young man. 'Edgbaston, that's what my name is. And that one over there – I know him well, we eat at the same fried trotter shop, on Eusebius Street it is, and very good value for the money – that one is called Edgeware. Edgeware Thackerwood, a bit of a mouthful. His mother and father were fond of riding the buses, you know. Ah, now we shall know, now we shall really know.' For the conductor had raised his stick, and the band, with the drums rolling beneath, crashed out with:

'Lets me out, that does,' said the man called Edgbaston. 'And old Edgeware too. Edgy!' he called. The man called Edgeware Thackerwood was gloomily reading a bit of old news-paper. He looked very much like Mr Gladstone of the Eden-borough Revue. He turned when he was called, nodded, and went off, Edgbaston following. Everybody was going off, so Edgar thought he would go off too. But the clown bounced towards him, crying:

'Didn't you hear the music? E and D and G and A. You have the look of a young fellow that fits in all right there. What's your name then?' Edgar told him. At once the clown roared it aloud, and there was a great noise of cheering, while the band began to play 'SEE THE CONQUERING HERO COMES'. The clown cried: 'Edgar! Edgar!' and the onlookers on the rim of the square, and the tourists with their cameras at the windows, joined in with a cry of 'Edgar!' And then a chorus of very pretty girls came on in a cart pulled by two old horses, while the band played a new tune, one that seemed to have been written for Edgar's own benefit, and the girls sang very sweetly:

> 'E and D and G and A
> And add an R to that.
> Edgar is the name you say,

75

You say and sing it every day,
But do not sing it flat.
E and D and G and A
Make quite a pretty tune.
But though you cannot sing the R
It's pleasant on a small guitar
Beneath a Spanish moon.'

While the singing was going on, Edgar was being gar-
landed with the most beautiful sweet-smelling flowers, of all the
colours of the Erckmann or Eridanian rainbow – malpacket,
lorenzo, elia, essene, williams, esplandian and pythagoras. Then
Edgar found himself being lifted on to strong shoulders of men in
white tracksuits and being borne off he knew not whither. He
called to the capering clown:

'Where? Where? Where?'

But there was no reply, except from the band, which
crashed out a very strange-sounding fanfare on the first four
letters of his name (try it on the piano or the electric organ or the
espriella, if you have one. But if you have a band sitting doing
nothing in the cellar playing cards all day long, give them all a
good clip on the ear, make them tune their instruments, and then
have them crash it out f f f, which means fortissimo, which means
very very loud):

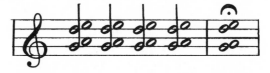

Edgar could hardly see where he was being taken, being so
smothered in flowers, but he soon found himself, to loud cheers
and band-noises, being carried inside a big cool building through
a great open doorway, and then he was plonked gently enough
down on a chair and the chair was at a long table, and the table was

76

The white-tracksuited men who had brought Edgar in now bowed themselves out, and Edgar was entirely on his own. The room was bare but full of doors, and it smelt vaguely of mint and lilies.

covered with the following marvellous eatables and drinkables:

An esto perpetua pie, very hot, with a jug of etzel cream next to it.

A fried Flemish sompnour, with euphelian potatoes.

Three singing euphrosynes, garnished with demogorgons and plain raw shredded cabbage.

A piece of beef done in the brasenose manner, stuck all over with little savoury pieces of knossos.

Braised slices of jocelyn in a rich cogglesby sauce.

A cold rice pudding.

Caladbolgs, very light and airy, with little stewed caliburns and caledvwlchs on toast done in the Excalibur style.

A great silver dish crammed with huibrechts and eyrbyggjas, all steaming hot.

Tea. Great Exhibition tea. Exeter tea (sometimes called Leofric leaf). Alfoxden tea. Lob-lie-by-the-fire tea. Jan of the Windmill tea. Ex pede Herculem tea. Examination of Sir William Hamilton's Philosophy tea. Evangeline tea. Eustace Diamonds tea. Eureka tea. Golden Legacie tea. Tea.

The white-tracksuited men who had brought Edgar in now bowed themselves out, and Edgar was entirely on his own. The room was bare but full of doors, and it smelt vaguely of mint and lilies. He had just taken a delicious huibrecht, the pastry light as the kiss of spring and the filling of hot waynflete jam pungently sweet, and was about to pour himself out a mug of Euphorion tea when one of the doors opened and two quiet figures came in. Edgar's mouth, still full of half-chewed huibrecht, opened nearly to the limit at the sight of them. One was a sort of lady and the other a sort of gentleman. But the gentleman spun round to show he had a face at the back of his head as well as at the front, and the lady seemed to be hopping on one leg. He couldn't actually see the leg, which was hidden by a long flowery skirt, but he assumed, from the jerkiness of her motion towards him, that she was a one-legged lady. She said:

'So sorry to interrupt your meal, my dear boy, but our entrance is part of the proceedings. My name is Mrs Echidna, and this is my son, poor boy, whom unkind persons insist on calling the Blatant Beast.' Her son, both of whose faces were sad and handsome, sadly nodded. He wore beautiful clothes of red velvet and twirled a short rolled umbrella in his left hand. His manner of progression involved many graceful twistings and turnings, so that nobody, apparently, could accuse him of hiding one of his faces.

Edgar could not speak. He merely made noises.

'So,' said the Blatant Beast, 'when you've finished eating that delicious-looking eyrbyggja, we will be on our way. The car is waiting outside.'

'Wherewherewhere?' Edgar spluttered.

'Oh, to the Castle,' said Mrs Echidna. 'You are, dear boy, by way of being our prisoner.'

CHAPTER VI

In the Castle

E DGAR KEPT saying to himself: 'It's a dream a dream that's what it is it's a dream I shall wake up soon and everything will be all right meanwhile it's a bad bad dream a nightmare' – which might seem to you a sensible thing to be saying, but the fact is that if you dream you are dreaming you may easily dream that you're waking up, and what you wake up to (in your dream, that is) is only another dream, and that could well be worse than the other one, if you see what I dream, I mean mean. Saying all this to himself, he found himself being led quite gently to a great shining motor-car (an Estrildis 90, very rare and very expensive), with a dwarfish-looking driver wearing a uniform and a peaked cap. Newspaper photographers took pictures, and Mrs Echidna and her son kindly posed smiling for these, and Edgar tried to scream: 'Get me out of here!' but no sound issued from his lips. There were also masses of tourists, being held back from getting too close by a cordon of charming policemen, and these clicked and whirred away with their still and movie cameras.

'It's all for the tourist trade,' Mrs Echidna said. 'A terrible bore, of course, but one has to earn a living somehow.' Then they got into the car, the Blatant Beast sitting at the front with the driver. This meant that he could talk to Edgar without turning round. As the car sped off amid the cheers of the crowd, the Blatant Beast said to Edgar:

'The face now looking at you and talking to you is called Rearface, while the other one, which is looking ahead and addressing the driver occasionally (his name, by the by, is Alberich), is called Foreface. I am usually called BB. All clear? Good.'

'What,' said Edgar in a fearful choking croaking whisper, 'are you going to do me?'

'Oh, you're not to worry,' said Mrs Echidna. 'They all escape, and then the newspapers have big headlines saying so, which also is supposed to be good for the tourist trade. When I say *all escape* I perhaps exaggerate a little. BB and I are quite willing to put everything which will enable you to escape at your disposal, but there's always the problem of my father, who's one of the old school. He doesn't believe in escaping, ah no. He believes in eating alive, bloodthirsty old cannibal as he is, if he'll forgive my saying so.'

'He's in Estotiland,' said BB's Rearface. 'He'll neither forgive nor not forgive, seeing that he's not here to hear.'

'Oh, but he's so *quick* about everything,' sighed his mother. 'Turn your back for an instant – me, I mean, not you, of course – and lo and behold he's there.' Edgar now saw that she did not after all have a single leg. She had instead a very powerful tail, muscular as a kangaroo's or perhaps a python's (though a python is all tail, except for its head – rather like a coin when you come to think of it), and Edgar remembered what the boatman had told him, so long ago it seemed: *Like a big snake from the waist down.* He should have felt more fearful than ever, but he did not: he was just full of pity and admiration for a lady who had to get around by balancing on the end of her tail. He looked at her

81

face: a *nice* face, with big round spectacles and ear-rings in the shape of Maltese crosses, and a little portrait of her son BB in a cameo brooch. The world was a hard place for everyone, and monsters were no exception. He now said:

'What's the name of your father, and er er what does he –'

'Look like?' said BB's Rearface. 'Grandfather is just big, that's all. Just very very very very big. A giant you could call him.' And then the Foreface, which Edgar of course could not see, addressed Alberich the driver: 'A giant, yes, Alberich?'

'Most is giants to the likes of me,' Alberich said. 'But that he's pretty big I'll not go so far as to deny.' And Rearface nodded to Edgar, as to indicate that what Alberich said made very good sense indeed.

'And what's his name?' again asked Edgar.

'Changes it a great deal,' Mrs Echidna said. 'According to who's in the news as having done something really bad. *Earthquake Strikes Nicaragua.* That's a what, not a who, but it makes no odds to my father. Mr Earthquake. He's a busy man. He's behind a lot of the bad things.'

'Well, let us hope that Estotiland keeps him busy for a time,' said BB-RF. 'Ever been there?' he said conversationally to Edgar. 'Interesting. A kind of Russian America or American Russia. Imagine that America has turned into Russia and Russia has turned into America and you have a good idea what it's like.' Edgar tried hard to imagine this but soon gave it up. He concentrated as best he could on the landscape outside the car window: lakes, volcanoes, forest, pig-pasture, the occasional village where they seemed to be making artichoke and beetroot wine. It seemed a long way to the –

'Ah, here it is – the Castle,' said BB's RF. 'Just coming to the hill now. Imposing, wouldn't you say? Terribly expensive to keep up, of course, but the Lord Mayor and Corporation of

Edgar could see what looked to him like a quite ordinary old house though a big one, with towers of different heights all stuck on to it – like a bunch of church candles that had been lighted at different times and then all put out at the same time.

Edenborough help. It's all tourist trade, you know. They come and see the place at week-ends, paying an entrance fee, of course, and also on public holidays like Aram, Etruria and Till Eulenspiegel's Anniversary. We allow them to see *just a little*, no more, but that seems to satisfy them so long as they can take photographs. People,' he said with gloom, 'are easily satisfied.'

Edgar could see what looked to him like a quite ordinary old house though a big one, with towers of different heights all stuck on to it – like a bunch of church candles that had been lighted at different times and then all put out at the same time. To add to the candle effect, wisps of smoke seemed to be arising from the tops of the towers, but this was probably coming from hidden chimneys. There were also pennants flying in the quite strong wind, and there was a moat and a flimsy-looking drawbridge. They now drove up to the drawbridge and the driver Alberich blasted a little tune on his three or four horns. The drawbridge was let down with a good deal of creaking, and some of the cables seemed to be very frayed. So they drove over the moat, and the drawbridge-operator greeted them with low bows and a long smile of few teeth. He seemed to be Alberich's brother or cousin. He settled down to quite a lengthy talk with Alberich.

'How was it then in the town?'

'All right. We've got the new one in the back here.'

'No rain? No snow? No weatherly extravaganzas?'

'As I always tell you, the weather's the same there as it is here.'

'In a great big town like that? Nonsense. It stands to reason they can afford better weather than that that we have.'

'But I've told you before, you don't pay for weather.'

'And *I've* told *you* before that you can't lay on one of these big thunderstorms without digging pretty deep in the pocket. Why, the lightning alone must cost a small fortune, quite apart

They now drove up to the drawbridge and the driver Alberich blasted a little tune on his three or four horns. The drawbridge was let down with a good deal of creaking, and some of the cables seemed to be very frayed.

from the thunder.'

'Look,' said BB wearily, 'we've had enough of all this, Bolingbroke. Alberich, drive on.'

'But he's got to be convinced, sir. He never seems to learn. Paying for weather, indeed.'

The creature called Bolingbroke first shook with anger and said: 'Everything has to be paid for, that's laid down, that is.' Then he became calm and smiling and said: 'I'll admit that when it rains stray cats and stray dogs there's no money involved. Giving them away they are, in a manner of speech. But sometimes you get real pedigree animals coming down – Persian cats and German shepherd dogs – and those cost a pretty penny, I can tell you. Bless you, it's all ignorance, but you'll grow out of it in time.'

'Drive on, Alberich,' said BB's two faces for greater volume. They drove on into the courtyard, and then the passengers got out, while Alberich drove further on, presumably to a garage.

'Well,' said Mrs Echidna, 'I suppose you'll want to see your room.'

Edgar found himself, and them, in a great entrance hall with a log fire burning in the huge fireplace, with pictures of ancestors and relations on the walls – he particularly noticed the Sphinx of Egypt – and ancient rusty weapons hanging between them – all too blunt, he thought, to cut butter when it was hot. From one of the many doors a man in a striped waistcoat appeared, whom Edgar took to be a sort of butler. He again seemed to be a brother or cousin of Alberich, judging from his appearance, and he came in grumbling.

'Ah, Etheredge,' BB's Foreface said, 'so there you are.'

'Well, it's certainly me,' Etheredge growled, 'and I'm certainly not nowhere else. What's your pleasure, not that it matters much?'

'Our *pleasure*,' said Mrs Echidna in ringing tones, 'is that you escort this young gentleman to his room. *At once.*'

'Hasn't got no luggage,' said Etheredge. 'Hasn't got much of anything, I'd say, getting himself kidnapped and brought here. No sense, that's certain. Well, you'd better come along of me, young shaver, and I'll show you what's what.'

'Supper,' said BB, 'will be in one hour's time.'

'Three hours, more like it,' said Etheredge. 'The cat ran off with the fish and the fox with the chicken. Cook's sitting there, wondering what to do. I told her to make pancakes even though it's Wednesday. She's thinking about it.' Then he made a rough come-with-me gesture with his head at Edgar.

Edgar was led up the fine wide stairs to a corridor full of doors. Everything had a smell of damp breadcrumbs. Etheredge grumbled all the time – about the pains in his feet, about his creaking bed, about the weather (sometimes too much rain, sometimes not enough), about the hard work which being a butler entailed. At length he pushed open a door and there was Edgar's room. Edgar gasped when he saw it. It held nothing except a chair, a table, a kind of television screen, and a sort of trap-door in the floor. 'There's no bed,' said Edgar.

'Of course there's no bed. It's not your job to waste time sleeping but to try and get out of here. You'll see how it all works when you've had your supper – if there is any supper, that is.'

'Well, what do I do between now and supper – if there is any supper, that is?' (Edgar added Etheredge's own words in a mocking manner.)

'Do?' Etheredge chuckled. He did not seem to mind the mockery. 'Before you get any supper at all you've got to do what they call the prelims. Know what those are?' Edgar didn't. 'Well,' Etheredge said, 'this here master of mine, Mr B. Beast,

87

used to teach in a school, you know. And useful he was, having two heads like he's got. When he was drawing or writing on the blackboard he could see what the young rascals was doing. When all the teachers except him was away ill with the affluenza he used to teach two classes at the same time – one in front, one behind. Marvellous I believe he was, one face teaching Spanish geometry and the other Swedish drill. Then he lost his job because there was something in the Education Laws that said that no schoolmaster was allowed to be two-faced. But he still loves a bit of education. So I locks this door on you,' said Etheredge, pulling a big bunch of keys from his back pocket, 'double-locking and thribble-locking it, and you gets down to it at that table over there. Then when you've done what's what you gets your supper – if there is any supper.' He chuckled and went out. Edgar heard the keys turning. The door was a big massive chunk of oak. There was no way of getting away. There was a window, and that was barred. He tried the trap-door, but that was locked too. The television screen, which stood just behind the table and chair, began to flash at him. He sat down.

READY? That word flashed huge on the screen. Edgar said 'Yes,' and the screen seemed to hear him. What it now had flashing on it was the following problem. WHERE WAS MOSES WHEN THE LIGHT WENT OUT? Very easy. Edgar smiled. He knew the answer to that one. He said: 'In the dark.' The television screen seemed pleased, for it flashed and flashed like a little firework display. Then a new problem appeared – white letters like fire on a background of blackest night: CHANGE BLACK TO WHITE IN SEVEN MOVES CHANGING ONLY ONE LETTER AT A TIME AND MAKING A DIFFERENT REAL WORD AT EACH MOVE. Edgar said: 'I can't do that in my head. I need to write it down.' The screen flashed: JUST THINK IT THATS ENOUGH. So Edgar thought out the changes and, to his astonishment, these appeared on the screen. It took him rather a long time, but he did it.

BLACK BLANK BLINK CLINK CHINK CHINE WHINE WHITE.

Again the television screen seemed pleased, for it gave another little firework display and there was even a noise like band music in the background. But now came a very difficult question: EXPLAIN HOW IT IS THAT PEOPLE CAN BOTH LIE AND NOT LIE AT THE SAME TIME. Edgar did not understand. He thought and thought, but nothing that made any sense came to his brain. The question remained on the screen, fire on blackness, like an accusation. Suddenly, for no reason that he could explain, he caught an image in his mind of King Solomon in the Bible, and he found himself saying: 'King Solomon said that all men are liars, but King Solomon was a man, therefore he was a liar, therefore he was not telling the truth, therefore all men are not liars, but King Solomon was a man, therefore he was not a liar, therefore he was telling the truth when he said that all men are liars, but King Solomon was a man, therefore he was a liar, therefore he was not telling the truth when he said that . . .' A great noise, like a mixture of tolling church bells and ship's sirens, came out of the television screen. Then it said, fire on black:

SUPPER IS READY.

And there at the door, in a minute or so, stood Etheredge, jangling his keys. 'Did all right, young shaver, by the looks of things,' he said. 'Me, I was never clever. But that's only what they calls the prelims. The real hard stuff comes when you've had your supper. Pancakes it is, as I said. So come on down to it.'

Edgar was led down the stairs into the entrance hall, and then into a large dining room where Mrs Echidna and BB were already seated. On the table was a wobbling big pile of steaming pancakes. Edgar was glad to see them, as that banquet in Edenborough had been snatched from him after the first mouthful. And he had still had no tea to drink. Nor was there any tea on this table. To Edgar's slight surprise the butler Etheredge sat down at the table, instead of standing and pouring wine or whatever butlers are supposed to do, and he was quick to grumble at the quality of the pancakes.

'Made with eggs they are,' he said, chewing one, 'whereas as is well known snow is the only stuff to use. Makes them light and airy snow does.'

'The only way to keep him quiet,' said BB sighing (and BB was now wearing beautiful evening dress; he was also putting pancakes into both faces at the same time, but in a very gentlemanly way, not in a greedy manner at all) 'is to tell a story. Perhaps, mother, you would oblige.'

'I'll be the one to do the obliging,' growled Etheredge. And at once he broke into the following:

'I had a little pancake once
And it was good and kind to me.
In intelleck it was a dunce,
It thought a year had fifteen munce,
And every quid had sixteen punce,
And kippers grew beside the sea –
But, ah, in matters of the heart
It was as faithful as a hound.
At each hard word its tears would start,
It sobbed like it would fall apart,
And when you slapped it good and smart
It used to grovel on the ground.
I'll tell you how it saved my life.
It was the last one on the dish
Served to me by my loving wife.
I went for it with fork and knife
But then it roared with rancour rife

Although it looked delish-
Ous. 'Oh, eat me not,' it yelled,
'For you have ate more than enough.
Your stomach is completely felled.'
It did not speak so good. I held
My peace and listened, half-compelled
To cease to gulp and gorge and stuff.
It was the twentieth on the dish
And I had read that number twenty,
Whether of flesh or fowl or fish
Or plates of soup or chunks of shish
Kebab or anything you wish
Was to the stomach more than plenty.
So then I found myself convinced:
If I had ate it I'd have died.
My choppers neither ground nor minced
That little pancake, and I winced
To think of it, since I'm aginst
That sort of suicide.
I kept the pancake as a pet
For more years than I care to name,
And he or she'd be with me yet
Through storm and sun and cold and wet
If, like a idiot, I'd not let
A dog get near, and oh he ate
My pet. Ah, sin, ah, shame.
My loving wife said: 'Why not get
Another one?' And then I set
My teeth and growled with grim regret:
'It could not be the same.
Ah, no. A million quid I'll bet
It could not be the same.
The same. The same.
It could not be the . . .'

'Enough, I think,' said Mrs Echidna gently. 'I observe
that you have been able, despite your singing of that sad song, to

get through at least eighteen of these pancakes. Enough is enough.'

At this moment, without knocking, Bolingbroke came in grinning with a yellow envelope in his hand. 'How's the weather in here?' he said 'Ah, nice and dry, anyways. Here's what's just come,' he said to Etheredge. Etheredge took the yellow envelope and left the room hurriedly, driving Bolingbroke before him with lively kicks, saying:

'I'll give you weather, coming in here interrupting me at supper and without knocking.' The door closed. The door opened again, and Etheredge came in again with the yellow envelope on a tray. He went up to BB and said:

'This appears to be a telegram, my lord. No bad news, I hopes.'

BB tore open the envelope. His face fell. His other face probably fell too, but Edgar could not see it. 'Very bad news,' both faces said. 'He's coming.'

'Oh,' said Mrs Echidna, 'you don't mean . . .'

'I do mean. I mean very much. Grandfather's coming. He also says he has quite an appetite, having eaten little in Estotiland. Oh dear.' Both mother and son looked sadly at Edgar, and even Etheredge allowed his face to drop.

'I'm not staying,' Edgar said. 'I'm getting out of here. I'm not going to be eaten.'

'Well,' said BB, 'the only way out is by the trap-door. If we let you out by the front door or the back door he'll catch you. He's very quick at picking up a scent. He'll go sniff sniff sniffing for you, then he'll grab you without a doubt. No, my boy, it's back to your room for you.'

'Then out through the trap-door?' asked Edgar eagerly.

'Not so simple,' said BB. 'That trap-door is electronically programmed only to open when you solve the Final Problem.

BB tore open the envelope. His face fell. His other face probably fell too, but Edgar could not see it. 'Very bad news,' both faces said. 'He's coming.'

And the Final Problem is going to take some time. It's very very tough.'

'I'll solve it,' said Edgar. 'I'll have to solve it.' And he stuffed a pancake into his mouth and went marching out of the dining-room. All this trouble just to get back to the classroom and then home for tea. Tea? He's just had supper.

CHAPTER VII

Albert Helps

EDGAR SAT waiting at the little table facing the television screen. It was getting dark outside now, but the only light in the room came from a single swinging blue bulb above and, of course, the glow of the screen itself. (Why *swinging*, by the way? I wrote that down without thinking, knowing somehow it was right. There must be a draught coming from somewhere. Ah yes – from a broken pane in that window over there. The wind must be rising. Perhaps there will be an expensive thunderstorm. Wait.) Suddenly words began to appear on the screen – slowly, one word at a time:

EXPLAIN THE THEORY OF RELATIVITY.

Edgar looked with his heart beating fast with fear. He had heard of this Theory of Relativity, like everybody else, but he had no true idea of what it was all about. His first instinct was to dash out of the room, down the stairs, out of the Castle, away, away, anywhere, hoping that by wishing hard, or by some other miracle, he would find himself back safely and cosily in the boring classroom, listening to an account of the Anglo-Saxon kings. But the door was locked and, to confirm the fact of his imprisonment, a great thick sheet of iron began to descend from the ceiling, covering the door. There was only one way out, and that was through the trap-door over there, and there was only one way to get that trap-door to open, and that was by doing what the television screen was asking him to do:

EXPLAIN THE THEORY OF RELATIVITY.

Suddenly he heard a violent squeaking. He looked about him and then on to the floor: the squeaking was coming from a little grey mouse. The mouse nodded at him, raised a paw in greeting, then began to run up his trouser-leg. Smiling sadly, Edgar took the tiny creature on to the palm of his hand and spoke to it.

'We're both prisoners,' he said. 'You a mouse and I a boy, but we're both locked forever in this room.'

'Stuff and nonsense,' said the mouse, in a small but resonant squeak. 'I go and come as I please. I have a hole over there, see, and through that hole I can visit the great outside world as often as I wish. My name, by the way, is Albert.'

'Pleased to meet you,' said Edgar. 'My name is – '

'No time for that nonsense now,' squeaked the mouse briskly. 'We have other fish to fry.'

'Fish?' said Edgar stupidly.

'You know what I mean. What it says up there. Relativity and so on. Sorry, stupid of me – I mean just Relativity. Good, we'll begin. First, what's the speed of light?'

'Look,' said Edgar. 'This is ridiculous. You're only a mouse. What do you know about – '

'Oh, don't waste time.' The mouse had leapt from Edgar's hand onto the table, and now it faced him sternly, squeaking in impatience. 'The speed of light is three hundred thousand kilometres a second. Right?'

'I suppose so,' Edgar said.

'Suppose nothing. It *is* so. To save having to use that big

The mouse nodded at him, raised a paw in greeting, then began to run up his trouser-leg. Smiling sadly, Edgar took the tiny creature on to the palm of his hand and spoke to it. 'We're both prisoners,' he said. 'You a mouse and I a boy, but we're both locked forever in this room.'

mouthful of numbers every time, they call the speed of light *c*.'

'Sea? See?'

'No no – *c*, *c*, *c*, *c*, the letter *c*. Is there anything faster than *c*? Come on, tell me – quick.'

Edgar was quite sure that there was nothing faster than the speed of light and he said so.

'Good,' said the mouse. 'Now let us suppose that a train is travelling at the speed of light. Just suppose. It couldn't happen, but suppose, *suppose*.'

'I'm supposing.'

'And on top of this train a man is running towards the front of the train. Can you see that? As in a film. A man being chased by policemen along the top of the train. This man wants to reach the driver of the train and kill him.'

'Why?' said Edgar.

'Oh, don't waste time,' the mouse squeaked, dancing up and down. 'Because the engine-driver was the man who committed the crime that this running man is being chased by the police for. Along the top of the train. Right?'

'I suppose so,' said Edgar.

'Now, this man is running at a speed of a thousand kilometres a second.'

'Impossible,' Edgar said.

'Impossible? When the train itself is moving at three hundred thousand kilometres a second? Use your brains, sir. Anyway, the point is that the speed of the man from the viewpoint of somebody watching the trains go by is – what? Come on, come on, come on.' And the little creature danced urgently up and down.

'The man's speed,' Edgar said, 'is the speed of the train plus the speed he's running – three hundred and one thousand kilometres a second.'

'Ah,' said the mouse. 'So you see, then – there's something moving faster than light. But you said there's *nothing* that moves faster than light.'

'So I was wrong,' Edgar said.

'No, not at all wrong,' said the mouse, who, since he gave his name as Albert, we shall now call Albert. 'Goodness,' said Albert. 'How the wind is rising. There's going to be a very costly thunderstorm before long. The point is,' continued Albert, 'it's a question of observers. It's not a question of the speed of light *not* being the fastest thing there is. It's a matter of who's looking – the observer that is. Everything's relative to him or to her, and that's why the whole caboodle is called Relativity.'

'The whole what?' said Edgar.

'Caboodle. Cafoffle. Eikon Basilike. Fadladeen. The whole thing so to squeak, I mean speak.'

'I see,' said Edgar, not seeing at all. And then there was a flare of lightning outside. 'The storm's beginning,' he said. Thunder followed, because the speed of sound is pretty slow compared with the speed of light (nothing faster than light, when all's said and done). And then the television screen flashed a message:

HURRY HURRY HURRY HE IS ON HIS WAY.

'Oh, no, no, no,' cried Edgar.

'The old man, eh?' said Albert, nodding at the screen. 'Well, we shall have you out of this room in an eleatic palatunate, or even sooner. The law of the speed of light has to be the same for everybody, so what we have to start doing is to bend space and time. So you get a rod that's one metre long, and how long is it?'

'One metre, of course,' Edgar said. The rain was coming down heavily now.

'No, no, no, no,' danced Albert. 'It would be one metre if

99

it were not in a moving system. If it's in a moving system it's –
ah, it's the square root of 1 minus the square of the velocity of the
moving system divided by the square of the speed of light.
Think that quickly and *see* it on the screen.'

Edgar did his best, and there it was, silver on black,
flashing away, though the lightning interfered with it a good deal:

$$\sqrt{1-v^2/c^2} \text{ of a metre}$$

'And,' said Albert, 'believe it or not, but if you get a clock
in a moving system, the distance between the ticks is not one
second, but just a bit more.' The thunder crashed and the rain
swilled down. And then there came a knock at the door, and a
gentle voice could be heard calling:

'Edgar? Edgar? Are you there, Edgar?' Edgar was too
terrified to reply. He just gulped and gulped. 'I know you're
there,' said the voice. 'And now I'm coming for you. With one
blow of my fist I'm going to smash down the door, and then you
and I are going to be together. Nice and cosy, you and I.' And
then the gentle voice became a great roar that drowned the
thunder, and Edgar heard a fist smashing through wood.

'Oh, it's mad, mad, mad,' he cried.

'Quick,' squeaked Albert. 'You'd better start saying what
the Theory of Relativity is all about. *Now.*'

'The Theory of Relativity,' began Edgar, 'says that, says
that, says that – '

'I'll be with you in a matter of seconds, Edgar,' said the
voice outside the door. 'I can't come in, of course, being much
too big, but I'll put my arm in and I'll feel around for you with
my fingers, and then I'll have you, and it's all going to be nice and
cosy.'

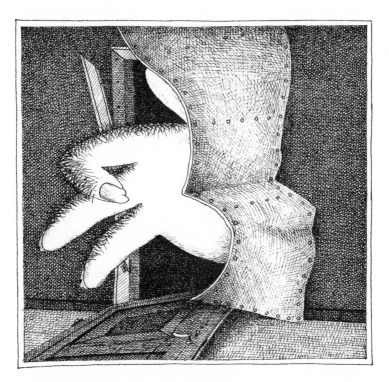

He looked back to see a hand pushing in from the broken entrance and twisted metal of the wall-door. The hand was feeling about, a very hairy hand with broken finger-nails. The hand was beginning to fill the whole room.

Lightning seemed to strike something somewhere, for Edgar heard a crash of toppling bricks and stone. Then spoke the thunder: 'Daaaaa!'

'Hurry,' said the dancing and very agitated Albert. And the television screen flashed:

HURRY HURRY HURRY.

'The speed of light,' Edgar said, his heart thumping so hard he could hardly hear himself think, 'is 300,000 kilometres a second for one observer, but it cannot be so for another observer moving away from the first observer. And yet we know that the speed of light *is* always the same. So we have to make changes for the observers themselves –'

'I've broken down the door,' cried the voice outside. 'Now I'm going to get to work on this big piece of iron. I'll chew through that with my teeth, I think.'

'Hurry hurry hurry,' squeaked Albert.

HURRY HURRY HURRY, flashed the television screen.

'This means,' gasped Edgar, 'that if somebody's running on top of a train that's moving at the speed of light, he thinks he's moving only at the speed he's running. But to somebody standing watching the train, he's running at c plus a thousand metres a second. It's a question of one thing being relative to one person, or observer, and another thing being relative to another. That's why it's called Relativity.'

'Owwwww,' roared the great voice. 'That hurt my front top teeth a bit, that did. Very tough metal, it is. But I shan't be long, my boy, I shan't be long at all. Owwwwww, terrible toothache.' The roar seemed to shake the whole house. The thunder, as in sympathy, roared too.

'Hurry hurry hurry,' roared I mean squeaked Albert.

HURRY HURRY HURRY HURRY HURRY.

'So,' gasped Edgar, 'the only way for the man watching

the man running on top of the train to see that man running at the speed of light and no more, because there is no more, is to make the seconds longer – the seconds in the moving system, that is, the train, that is. Something like that.'

'What you mean,' squeaked Albert, 'is that space gets shorter in a moving system and time gets longer.'

'What I mean is,' said Edgar, and then, to his immense relief, he saw the trap-door moving. The heavy door began to rise, and there was the sound of sweet music, as if to welcome him to freedom.

'Good luck,' squeaked Albert. 'Ah, I can see his fingers. I'd better get back to my hole.' And he ran, while Edgar cried his grateful thanks. Edgar himself now ran and prepared to enter the opening revealed by the risen trap-door. He looked back to see a hand pushing in from the broken entrance and twisted metal of the wall-door. The hand was feeling about, a very hairy hand with broken finger-nails. The hand was beginning to fill the whole room.

'I'll get you now. I'm feeling around for you. Ah, what a lovely time you and I are going to have together, Edgar.'

Edgar could see only darkness ahead of him. He entered it, his feet groping for stairs. But there were no stairs – only a long smooth chute. He shot down, sliding through the darkness.

CHAPTER VIII

Straight Through a Hole in the Desk

DARK DARK dark dark dark, and a great wind roaring, but the thunder and rain were at the back of him and growing fainter. And then a hint of light, a glimmer of light, a glow of light, and there he was blinking in the light of day, though when he had started to slide down the chute it was already evening. He looked around him and saw thousands of people milling around, happy and excited, though some of the children were crying with over-excitement, and they were all dressed in a very old style – the women with huge bustling skirts and the men in grey top hats, carrying canes. He looked behind him to see the hole through which he had appeared slowly closing up and becoming part of the surface of a smooth wall. He looked up and saw a great roof of glass with the sun shining through. And then a tall man spoke to him. He said:

'What strange clothes you're wearing, boy. Are you part of the Exhibition?'

'What exhibition, sir?' asked Edgar, ready, now that he was safe, to be very polite and kind and smiling to everyone.

'Why, the Great Exhibition, of course,' laughed the man. 'Do you hear that, Martha?' he said to his plump little wife. 'Do you hear that, Laetitia, Eugenia, Mary, Phoebe, Vicky, Ermintrude, Gertrude, Annie, Chloe, Alberta?' he said to his many daughters. 'This young fellow said *What exhibition?*' They all laughed, though quite pleasantly. 'Why, this is the Greatest Exhibition the world has ever seen,' said the man. 'There's everything here. You need a railway train to take you round it.'

A railway train at once came chuffing up, and the driver and the stoker were none other than Bob Eccles and Boniface, the two sailors who had rowed Edgar from the ship to the island. 'Get in the cab with us, young un,' said Boniface. 'And sing us a song to keep us in trim for the engine-driving.'

'Where is er the er young er lady?' Edgar asked. 'Rhoda something.'

'Rhoda Fleming?' cried Boniface. 'Why, she's still there criticising. Doesn't like being in the dark at all, so I opened up my shirt a bit as you can see for her to peep out. Come on, then, climb aboard young un.'

Edgar was only too happy to be there in the cab, burning hot as it was and full of steam and oily metal. Off they went, chuffing away, and Edgar sang:

> '*With the coke and the smoke and the choke of oil*
> *And the wheels go round like a dream,*
> *For despite the task and its terrible toil*
> *And the heat so hot that you nearly boil*
> *And the piston's thrust and its tough recoil,*
> *There is nothing nicer than steam.*'

And Bob Eccles and Boniface came in with the chorus:

> '*And you tap the wheels to see if they're cracked*
> *When the wheels are not going round,*
> *But some come out with a contrary fact –*
> *It's to see if the wheels are sound.*'

The tiny voice of Rhoda Fleming came squealing from inside her

A railway train at once came chuffing up, and the driver and the stoker were none other than Bob Eccles and Boniface, the two sailors who had rowed Edgar from the ship to the island. 'Get in the cab with us, young un,' said Boniface. 'And sing us a song to keep us in trim for the engine-driving.'

owner's shirt: 'Far too much sound. I can't hear myself squeal.'

They all ignored her, especially as they had just arrived at the platform of a small railway station, where Mr Eckermann and Mr Eckhart and the little man who helped them in the office on the pier were dancing up and down, a parrot squawking and fluttering over their heads. 'You can't get off here!' they shouted. 'There's no ticket collector.' And a tiny voice cried:

'Hector pecked her.'

'We'll see your passports, though,' said the little man, 'seeing as you've got here.'

'Ah, no,' growled Boniface. 'Not if you're not letting us ashore. You can't have it both ways.'

And then a horse thundered on to the platform from an opening marked WAY OUT. There was a lady on it cracking a whip. She called in a deep voice: 'Come on, you. *Jildi, hitherao,* or I'll thrash you within an inch of your life, you lump of lazarooshian leather, you.' And then the little Indian appeared, saying:

'My goodness, I am trying to get chocolate out of the chocolate machine, *missi sahib.*'

'Never mind about that now. We've got to get on board this train here. I don't see any van for the horse,' she frowned.

'No getting aboard,' said Mr Eckermann or Mr Eckhart. 'There's no ticket-collector and there's no ticket-seller neither.' And both Mr Ecks waved the train away.

'Come on then,' said Bob Eccles. 'On us way.' And off they went. There was now a lot of dancing with rage on the platform, and the voice of the Indian could be heard very distinctly:

'Oh goodness gracious, I have to be being in Bombay, yes, and no more trains till further notice.' The lady began to whip him, but he always got out of the way of the stroke.

'I'm terribly thirsty,' said Edgar, and he was too, what with the heat and the coal-dust. Boniface said:

'Well, if you care to climb back over that coal-tender there, you can get on the train through the roof, and you'll find what they call a refreshment-car somewhere or other.'

Edgar found the baker-woman and Mr Quimby sitting among the chunks of coal. Mr Quimby was eating bits of coal with great relish and covering his face with coal-dust. 'Delicious,' he said. 'And very well cooked, if I may say so, ma'am.'

'It's only coal,' said the baker-lady, 'and I think you're ridiculous.'

'Ah, but it's all in the mind,' Mr Quimby said. 'In my mind this is delicious turkey and cranberry sauce and pumpkin pie. Yum yum,' he went, crunching at a shining black lump with apparent enjoyment. Neither of them took any notice of Edgar. Edgar crawled over the coal and, on the leading carriage, saw there was a kind of trap-door with a gentleman dressed like Shakespeare leaning out. On his shoulder there was a mouse dressed in old-fashioned lady's clothes. Edgar remembered both of them well. Mr Eden said:

'It's not possible that we're going where they say we're going, for it's not on the map yet. Therefore there's no such place.'

'Sure, sorr,' said the mouse called Maria, 'and isn't it yourself that's after taking the words out of my mouth itself?'

'Hallo,' said Edgar. 'How are you both? I've met a mouse called Albert – awfully clever. Any relation of yours?'

'Ah, well now, sorr, with a name like Albert he was bound to go far in his fizzology and his didicology and all the rest of the rigmarole.'

'No such place,' Mr Eden kept grumbling. Edgar was kindly allowed to enter the train by the roof (the train was certainly not travelling at the speed of light – WHICH IS WHAT, BY THE WAY? DO YOU REMEMBER? YOU DON'T? JUST YOU WAIT TILL YOU'VE FINISHED READING THIS STORY – I'LL· BE THERE WAITING FOR YOU – nothing like it).

Edgar found himself inside a compartment full of thin gloomy men with little gold crowns on. They were all bearded and had plenty of hair, as well as little gold crowns on their heads. Their bodies were mostly covered in chain-mail. One of them said:

'You've entered feet first, I see. It would have been more entertaining for you to come in head first.' Another one came out with a kind of growling piece of verse:

> *'Cometh in head first, falleth on feet,*
> *Feet first he falleth, forelock in air,*
> *Maketh no difference the way he doth cometh.'*

'But that's *terrible*,' said another man, 'My dear Eadward the Elder, you have a lot to learn about your own dear Anglo-Saxon language.' Edgar was suddenly filled with awe. He said:

'Are you – sirs – your majesties – the Anglo-Saxon kings of England?'

'We most certainly are,' said Eadward the Elder. 'There's Eadmund Ironside, and there's Eadred, and there's Eadward the Confessor, and there's – oh, I can't be bothered with all the names.'

'I was learning all about you at school,' Edgar said.

'Really?' said Edward the Confessor, looking really pleased. 'So they teach all about us at school, do they? Well, that's what I'd call fame. When we were at school there was absolutely nothing taught about us. That is what they call progress, I suppose.'

'Boy,' growled Eadward the Elder, 'you can bring in

foaming ale in alecups for us, or else mead in a mazer, and look sharp about it.'

'I,' said Edgar proudly, 'am not a servant, your majesty. I'm a free boy.'

'You are, are you?' said Eadward the Elder, much politer now and sounding rather interested. 'A new idea, that – free boys. Well, I suppose it had to happen sooner or later.'

'We seem to be there,' said Eadmund Ironside, who had big bent sheets of rusty iron on his sides. 'This is supposed to be the best part of the Great Exhibition.'

'What is it?' Edgar asked.

'Beasts. Monsters. Giants. That sort of thing.' The kings spoke in turn, getting up yawning as the train puffed into the station. They took it in turn to settle their crowns on their heads and to comb their beards with their fingers, using the one little mirror set below the luggage-rack on the side of the compartment nearest the engine.

Edgar did not like the sound of all this at all. He had just escaped from a giant, and he did not want to meet any more monsters, even ones as nice as the Blatant Beast and his mother. 'All I want,' he said, as he was jostled out on to the platform, 'is to get back into the classroom.' Nobody seemed interested. 'To learn all about the Anglo-Saxon kings,' he added. Then they all smiled and puffed themselves up, and one or two said: 'Good good good.' But they did not seem interested in suggesting ways of getting back to the classroom. King Eadmund (940-946) said:

'Work hard at this king business and, who knows? – perhaps you'll have lessons given about *you*. Better to be taught about than to be taught. I say – that's rather good.' He tried to repeat the phrase to his namesake Ironside, but that rusty-flanked man was not inclined to listen. There was a lot of jostling.

The platform was crowded, and everybody seemed to be

Edgar saw, with sympathy, how the Edenborough
Revue was trying to draw the crowd away from the
theatre to watch its own little show, which it was
trying to present on top of a pile of chicken-crates and
mailbags.

trying to get into a large theatre whose entrance was in the station itself. Edgar saw, with sympathy, how the Edenborough Revue was trying to draw the crowd away from the theatre to watch its own little show, which it was trying to present on top of a pile of chicken-crates and mailbags. He heard Tommy Carlyle lamenting:

'Och aye, lads, it's the way o' the worrrld. They dinna ken the guid when they see it.' Then he was knocked off his chicken-crate by a couple of bullies, jostling towards the theatre entrance. Edgar didn't want particularly to go into the theatre, for he did not consider that that was the way home (meaning to the classroom, with home afterwards), but he was so pushed and pulled by the crowd, which was mostly dressed in the style of the days of Good Queen Victoria (may heaven send her peace, but she couldn't compare with our own Queen Edith Swan Neck), that he was forced into the huge hall – which must have had room for about ten thousand people – and kept on being forced forward towards the front. (The best seats were in the middle and back, but these were mostly already taken.) And then who should come bustling towards him, hitting other members of the crowd out of the way (they didn't like this: one old crocodile in a bonnet, little crocodiles holding on to her skirts, cried: 'This is no way to treat a lady, young man') but the dog who had called himself King Edwin of Northumberland. Edwin at once told the crocodile: 'We'd know how to deal with the likes of you where I come from, which is Northumberland, and I'll trouble you to call me Your Majesty, old crocodile as you are.' Then he said to Edgar: 'Come. We've got the best place in the whole house all lined up for you, my boy.'

He grabbed Edgar with a very horny paw and led him through a door which said EXIT and kept on saying it ('Exit exit exit exit') and down a long corridor and through another door which said nothing, then up some stairs, then to a place with huge red velvet curtains at one end, and all the time Edgar was breathlessly trying to say: 'Why where what who.'

'Ah,' said Edwin, 'you'll be giving pleasure and profit to thousands. The stage – the theatre – the glamour of the grease-paint and the terror of the footlights – if only I'd not been king I'd have been ready for those myself, you know. Sometimes, in my gorgeous palace, waited on forepaw and hindpaw by bowing servants, I dream of the life I missed. The stage.'

'You sell cold drinks for a living,' said Edgar.

'Do I? Do I?' growled Edwin. 'Ah, they're here for you now.' And there appeared two people Edgar had not wished to see again, even though they had done him no real harm – Mrs Echidna and her son the Blatant Beast. BB said (and he was wearing a very smart suit of silk that glistened and sparkled and waved like moonlit water):

'I don't think there's any need to tell you how really deeply both mother and I regret all this. But he would insist, you see. *Thwarted* was the word he used, wasn't it, mother?'

'*Thwarted*,' agreed Mrs Echidna very sadly. 'He would never allow himself to be *thwarted*. It's all most regrettable, but we have to think of the tourist trade. He'd tear the Castle down, of that I'm quite sure, and as for what would follow – ' She shook her head and wobbled on her snake-tail as though likely to faint with the horror of what might happen after the tearing down of the Castle. 'But he's agreed to give you a run for your money, if that's the right expression.'

'Really,' said Edwin, 'for the money of those who've paid to come in and watch.'

'Treachery,' cried Edgar. 'Ghastly horrible treachery. I'm getting out of here.'

'Ah, no, you're not,' said BB's two faces with genuine

regret. And he gestured to behind Edgar. Edgar turned to see a whole army waiting, led by a French king who cried '*Pour l'honneur de la France.*'

'There are plenty of kings around,' said Edgar. 'I'll say that.'

And then there was loud music from a brass band, a fanfare which Edgar already knew, for it consisted of the first four letters of his name.

'*Allez,*' called the French king, '*a la gloire.*'

'That,' said the dog-king Edwin, 'means *go to glory*. We used to have a lot of French spoken in Northumberland. Well, then, now, you sir, you're to go on stage.' The two dwarf servants, Bolingbroke and Etheredge, cackled, and then they pulled the curtain apart, and then Edgar tottered on to the stage.

There was loud clapping as he appeared. He blinked out into the darkness, wondering whether he ought to bow. But he was too upset, though not now very much frightened (let's get it over with, he kept telling himself), to put on a good stage performance. And he was also amazed to see what the stage scenery consisted of. It seemed to him at first vaguely familiar, then it seemed more familiar, then at last it was wholly familiar. It was the inside of his school desk.

It was the inside of his school desk, only magnified hundreds of times, so that – if this had really been the inside of his school desk he would have been no bigger than a fly. He knew it was the inside of his school desk because of the smell – only the smell too was greatly magnified. There was not only the usual smell of ink and of sharpened pencils, but also the smell of apples and oranges. There were not only those smells, but also the smell of a pet mouse he had once kept in his desk. And, finally, there was the smell of some candy he had had once that nobody else had had, because his uncle George Percival had brought it him all the

And he took his pipe out of his mouth and put a silver whistle there. He blasted three times shrilly. At once the ship flew like a bird out of the pages of the book.

way from Slobovia – a smell of what the candy had been made of. It had been made of honey and aniseed and citron and cloves and had had a faint sprinkling of curry powder on it.

He could tell what the books were too: by walking along their spines he could read the titles: ELEMENTARY ASTROPHYSICS & MATHEMATICS FOR INTELLIGENT BOYS AND GIRLS. HISTORY MADE NOT EXACTLY EASY BUT LESS DIFFICULT THAN IT NORMALLY SEEMS TO BE. And one book was wide open at an illustrated page. Edgar could not tell what the picture was – it was far too big – but he could see certain words, each letter bigger than himself, attached to the picture: *CRO'JACK* was one word, and *MIZZEN* was another. What did the words mean? He used to know, or so he thought, but he knew no longer. And then he heard the voice . . .

'Ah, Edgar. I missed you before, but I shan't miss you this time. All I have to do is to open this silly little desk, and there you'll be waiting.'

The voice came from above, and, miles above it seemed, Edgar saw the lid of his desk. He saw it from the inside, a view completely new to him. He could even see a hole in the lid. Was that the hole he had crept into so long ago? If he were really a fly, instead of merely the size of one, he could buzz up there and escape from the desk. But up there he would meet . . . Oh, no, no. And yet, if he were really a fly, he could fly away and miss the huge groping murderous hands.

'I'm coming now, Edgar. It would make things a lot easier for me if you'd sit on the cover of one of your books – say, METAPHYSICS FOR THE VERY YOUNG – and then I could pick you up without trouble.'

The audience seemed to be enjoying the show very much. There was appreciative laughter and a kind of quiet hum of excitement. And then Edgar heard something other than the voice. It came from the book with pictures in it. It was the sound of the sea and the wind roaring. Then Edgar remembered what those words *cro'jack* and *mizzen* meant. They had something to do with the parts of a sailing ship. And then a new voice called, from inside the book itself:

'Heave ho, my hearty? Your name's on the sailing list. Get aboard yarely, for the anchor's weighed.'

Edgar scrambled into the book just as he saw the huge lid of the huge desk creaking open. There was a sailing ship ready to leave the harbour. But there was no gang-plank. How did he get on board?

'Shan't be half a second now, Edgar,' came the huge voice from above. 'I'm just going to dip my hand in.'

Edgar saw, on the deck of the ship, an old man, all white beard and oilskins, a red-coaled pipe held firm in smiling jaws. 'Here it is,' he called. 'Coming down now.' And a rope-ladder came hurtling down from the deck. Edgar grasped it and began to climb.

'Hm, Edgar, that's naughty. You're not where I told you to be.' He climbed and climbed and climbed. 'Very naughty. I can't see you at all. Oh, why do you make things difficult for an old man like me?' There was a murmur of sympathy from the audience.

But now Edgar was on the deck, the captain puffing smiling pipesmoke at him. 'Are we safe, sir?' gasped Edgar.

'You just watch this,' said the old man. 'Hold on tight, everybody. All hands to ship's stations.' And he took his pipe out of his mouth and put a silver whistle there. He blasted three times shrilly. At once the ship flew like a bird out of the pages of the book.

'Blast my white whiskers,' said the captain, looking up. 'The lid's up. That hole isn't there any longer.' Then he saw the groping gigantic hand. He called: 'Master gunner!'

'Aye aye, sir!'

Suddenly a cannon boomed, and Edgar saw a little black ball sailing through the air somewhat faster than the ship. There was an explosion and a cry of pain. The lid of the desk slammed shut like all the thunder in the world. A voice as loud as the thunder yelled:

'That hurt, that hurt, that hurt – owwwwwwwwww!' There was the sound of applause from the audience.

'Here we go,' said the captain. 'Straight through.' And the ship entered the tunnel and sped through the darkness. 'Time to say goodbye, I suppose,' the captain said. Edgar could see his face faintly in the glow of his pipe. 'Never got to know your name, but it was pleasant enough having you aboard. And now I give you a bit of a push . . .'

Edgar came through the hole in the desk to hear Mr Anselm Eadmer, his teacher, droning on about Anglo-Saxon royalty. Edgar saw himself very big, with his eyes closed, sitting at his desk. He ran over the surface of the desk towards this big Edgar and gave him a pinch in the left hand. Big Edgar's eyes opened. Little Edgar crawled up big Edgar's arm, swift as a mouse, on to his neck, up to his ear. He entered his ear. Big Edgar and little Edgar became one and the same person.

'Edmund Ironside,' Mr Eadmer said. 'So-called because of his great strength and bravery and fortitude. You there, Edgar, are you awake, or are you dreaming of Easter eggs? The Easter holiday hasn't started yet, boy.'

'I was awake, sir,' said Edgar. 'He was called Eadmund, not Edmund. And he was called Ironside because he had these very rusty sheets of iron fixed to his sides.'

The rest of the class laughed. Mr Eadmer smiled grimly. 'Ah, our friend Edgar has some special source of knowledge, I see.

All right, no need to laugh. He was right about the *Eadmund,* anyway. And I don't care where he got the knowledge.' He wrote on the blackboard, in very large and clear block capitals, the name EADMUND. 'That's the Anglo-Saxon form of the name. And the Anglo-Saxon form of Edgar's name would be – ' He wrote it: EADGAR.

So, Edgar thought, if I'd told them my name was really *Eadgar* that tune the band played in Edenborough wouldn't have been the right one for me at all, and I wouldn't have had to go to the Castle and be so frightened and – But it's all over now.

The bell rang. The lesson was over. School was over. Term was over. The Easter holidays were beginning. But Mr Eadmer was not one of these schoolmasters who rush out of the classroom, sometimes even in the middle of a sentence, when the bell rings. He said:

'Any other information you can give us about anything, Edgar or Eadgar? Anything else from the land of dreams? Einstein's Theory of Relativity, for instance?' The class laughed, as they all knew that the Theory of Relativity was the hardest thing in the world. They mostly turned to look at Edgar and have a good laugh at him. But Edgar said:

'Certainly, sir. The Theory of Relativity has something to say about the speed of light – three hundred thousand kilometres a second usually represented by the symbol c. If light maintains this velocity for one observer, it cannot do so for another observer who is moving away from the first observer with a certain additional velocity – not unless we establish the principle of relative space and time . . .'

The class was silent now. It looked at Edgar with wonder and a certain fear. Mr Eadmer was silent, also thoughtful. He said:

'You must take me with you sometime, Edgar or Eadgar.

On one of these dreamy trips of yours. All right, class dismissed.
A happy Easter, everybody.'

'Happy Easter, sir.'

And Edgar at last was able to go home for tea. He hoped
there would be fish-paste sandwiches and cherry cake. He knew
there would be a nice hot pot of tea. He was very thirsty, also a
little tired. But after tea he would be lively again and ready to go
to the cinema. There was a good film on tonight at the Rialto –
something warlike and exciting about one of the Anglo-Saxon
kings of England.